DEFENDING NO WHERE

e a lake

Copyright © 2016 e a lake

All rights reserved.

ISBN: 1535270896

ISBN-13: 978-1535270892

This book is a work of fiction. The names, characters, places and incidents are products of the writer's imagination or have been used fictitiously and are not to be construed as real. Any resemblances to persons living or dead, actual events, locales or organizations are entirely coincidental.

All events portrayed are made up in the authors mind. As such, none are real. However, they are intended to give the reader pause to consider what a alternate future may look like. And since I get to make that future up in my head, some things just aren't going to make sense to everyone. Too bad.

All rights reserved. No part of this book may be used or reproduced in any form whatsoever without written permission of the author.

Also by e a lake:
WWIV - In The Beginning,
WWIV - Hope in the Darkness,
WWIV - Basin of Secrets, and,

WWIV - Darkness Descends (The Shorts - Book 1),
WWIV - Darkness's Children (The Shorts - Book 2).

Stranded No Where (Book 1: The No Where Apocalypse)
Surviving No Where (Book 2: The No Where Apocalypse)

<u>Coming Soon:</u>
Searching No Where (Book 4: The No Where Apocalypse)

For my father, Jim Stevens.
In No Where he would have known just what to do.

"Sometimes you have to travel a long way to find what is near..."

—*Dinesh Kumar Biran*

DEFENDING NO WHERE

Day 1,000

Bones! I'd found bones in Dizzy's backyard. In the spot where he had told me, once upon a time, that his dad was buried.

"What a moron," I whispered, checking quickly to be sure I was alone. I was.

Marge was with me, but she didn't want to take part in the actual burial. According to her, seeing Dizzy's charred remains would have been too much for her to handle. After I'd finished and covered the hole, then, and only then, would she come out and pray for our friend's soul.

I wiped my brow with a red-checkered handkerchief Lettie had given me a few years back. The sun was blazing hot for early May. Or at least what we thought was early May. Truth was, we had no idea.

Nate, Marge's youngest, had spent the last of the winter months trying to figure out how long everything had been gone. According to the rotted tires and rusting body of my Jeep, it had been plenty long enough. But the ugly times marched on, with no hope or end in sight.

According to Nate, we were at Day 1,000 of the apocalypse. Or somewhere close. He called it May 9th. I had no better information to go off of and not a lot of extra time on my hands, so I agreed.

Unlike my young friend, I had spent the last of the snows plotting my revenge against the people responsible for Dizzy's death. The plan was simple: find them, kill them. Every last one of them. All I needed was their location. With any luck, I'd have that within a week or two.

I poured the sack of remains into the sandy dirt, covering my face as they fell. For something six weeks old, they sure stunk. Only a small amount of flesh remained of Dizzy, just a little on his skull. Most had been burned away, while various northwoods creatures scavenged the rest. It didn't seem to me like a proper ending to such a unique character. But we were living in different times and had been for almost four full years. And would, I believed, for at least the rest of our days on Earth.

"You almost done?" Marge called out from the door of Dizzy's dilapidated trailer. Poor thing, I knew what she found inside wasn't pretty or flattering. But she claimed to know what she would discover.

I grabbed another shovelful of dirt. "Just got to cover it!" I shouted back.

Almost time to say one last goodbye my friend, I thought, watching the earth sift through what was left of his ribcage. *I will get them for this, Dizzy. I promise you that.*

Joining Marge inside, I waited for my eyes to adjust from the bright sun. The trailer was just as crappy as I'd remembered. Nothing that a gallon of gas and a match wouldn't fix.

She paged through some of Dizzy's unique collection of reading material — not that I believed he really read much.

"He certainly had interesting tastes," she said in a tone that was less foul than expected. "Most of these women have huge breasts. Not that many of them look very natural."

She peeked over at me. "I wonder what he saw in me." She held up a page with a picture of a large-breasted blonde and I grinned. "I'm far from this size."

"I think he found the natural beauty you have to be too undeniable," I replied, plopping on a spot of the dusty couch. "He always claimed he'd never come back here once he found you. Some consolation in that, I suppose."

She seemed un-offended. "Tom loved me and was honest about his past." She spread her arms wide. "Even all of this. Though there's more here than I expected to find."

"I'm sorry he's gone, Marge." God, I was pathetic. She was still hurting from his loss, and for the past six weeks, all I could ever say was the same old line.

At least this time it hadn't brought her to tears as usual. She nodded ever so briefly. "I know. And I know you miss him too, Bob. He was a good friend to all of us. And a pretty decent boyfriend for me."

Well, that was certainly true. He doted on the woman like no other I had ever seen. If she got up to fetch a glass of water, Dizzy always beat her to it. She needed a blanket, it was delivered with a smile and a small kiss. If she ever needed a hug, there he was. Hell, many times I wanted Dizzy to take care of *me* like that.

"What are we going to do with this place?!" she exclaimed, flinging cupboard doors open.

I sighed. The truth seemed so cold. "Scavenge it," I finally replied, rising to help her look for anything valuable. "After that," I eyed her cautiously, "probably burn it to the ground so no one else moves in close. No one bad at least."

I felt arms wrap around my waist; small shakes from her body echoed through mine. I placed my hands atop of hers.

"I'll make them pay," I whispered, feeling her head nod against my back. "They'll all pay. I promise you that."

Day 1,000 - continued

Chatting as we strolled, the two-plus mile walk took no time at all. We talked about Dizzy — Tom, as Marge called him — and all of his unique qualities. We covered Violet and her new arrival, Hope. We agreed she was the most beautiful thing in our world, and probably would be for a long, long time. We even spoke about our feelings of being left in a world that had so little to offer.

And we had plenty of little.

The sun felt good on my face and bare arms. Winter, again, had lasted far too long. Lettie said it always did here in Michigan's Northern Peninsula. Almost four years in and I still wasn't used to it.

My stomach grumbled, reminding me of our most pressing issue. I needed to take a deer, and soon. Soups with acorns and fiddlehead ferns weren't enough to hold me over anymore.

Turning off Dizzy Drive, I noticed people on the road in the direction of our cabin. Studying them carefully, eyes never leaving them, I slipped my 45 from behind my back. We hadn't seen but a few people since the snow melted.

Nevertheless, any stranger was a potential danger to us.

I eased my grip when I recognized Daisy's smile. I should have known it was her just based on that stupid sunbonnet she loved to wear. It had to be the only one in existence…with the exception of Libby's that matched her mother's.

"How'd everything go?" Daisy asked as we met and stopped. Her arms wrapped around Marge, giving her the comfort I couldn't. "I'm so sorry, Marge. We all miss Dizzy."

When Daisy said, "We miss Dizzy…" and "…so sorry…" it sounded so sincere, so real. I could say the same exact words, but it always sounded terrible coming from me. But she was a better person than I, in so many ways. That was merely one.

Exchanging a few pleasantries, my eyes wandered further down the road, some quarter mile past my cabin. The two figures in the east ditch looked familiar. I imagined the tall one was Nate. Libby was likely the other, which could only mean one thing.

"We should get back," I said, trying to turn Daisy. She resisted. I was right. "I need some water." I tried to make it sound like an urgent request. Still, she blocked my way.

"Let me guess…" I continued, my face twisting as I spoke.

Daisy raised her delicate hands and placed them on my chest. "She's just being a little fussy, that's all," she said, sounding sweeter than a girl accepting her first date. "And poor Vi got a little teary. So great-grandma Lettie is trying to smooth things over."

Tight-lipped and tense, I shook her words away. Marge gave Daisy's arm a squeeze and hustled home where she was undoubtedly needed.

"This is getting old," I said, watching a screeching blue jay hop from branch to branch in a dead pine. "That little thing screams more than anything else."

Daisy hugged me, as if she thought that would help. "Oh, it's not that bad, Bob."

I pointed down the road. "Then why are Nate and Libby nowhere near the house?" I had her, and could sense she knew it as well.

"Lettie says Vi's milk hasn't come in fully yet," Daisy explained smoothly, still holding me in place. That meant the screaming was in the world ending range. Whether baby or mother was the screamer was yet to be seen. "And poor Hope gets more air than nourishment. She needs another alternative, Hope does. Maybe real milk would help? She hardly ever drinks any water."

I recalled the night the tiny girl came into our lives, some two or three weeks back. Lettie thought at first Violet had enough milk. And then she didn't. Forcing as much water as we could down the mother's throat helped a little at first, and then it didn't. We couldn't catch a break the past few months.

We had one baby bottle, something Marge found stuffed in some old medical supplies she'd brought. Two diapers and a bunch of rags weren't going very far. And now, the complete demise of a mother and her milk, the lifeline that could keep the baby alive…and quiet. This really wasn't my problem, but my housemates — and the woman I loved — made it mine.

We all feared yet never spoke of the same thing. I could see it in every other adult's eyes, and was sure they could see it in mine. Heck, even Nate had to have known and wondered what we all did. Just how long could a baby survive on little more than love?

The solution to our worries required a long dangerous walk on my part, one that I'd put off for the past week. Now I had no choice. An innocent baby needed my help. Hope needed me.

Day 1,002

"So you go back past Dizzy's place until the road ends…" Lettie instructed, drawing at the same time. I already knew where the Wilson place was. I needed different information.

"Am I gonna get shot, Lettie? That's what I really need to know." She glanced up at me and tightened her lips. Not exactly the response I was hoping for.

"Probably not," she answered, stroking her lower lip with a pencil-thin finger. "Wilson's an okay fellow, once you get to know him. Just announce yourself right off and raise your hands up nice and high."

Clutching at my forehead, I moaned, "That's just great. I've lived through all of this only to get shot by Hope's grandfather. Just freaking great."

Marge and Daisy approached. "I made a list," Marge said enthusiastically, handing me a piece of paper. "Be sure to get some kind of milk, either cow or goat. Eggs would be good; Lettie says he has a large bunch of chickens. He may have jerky, too. That would be nice. And anything else that he might want to share."

The two younger adult women stared at me as I studied the

list. Both had stupid smiles plastered on their faces. Like that helped.

"You think I'm running to the grocery store?" I asked, perhaps a little terser than intended. But come on, what were they thinking?

"If he's got flour, get some of that, too," Lettie added, staring off into the woods. "A person can do a whole lot with a little bit of flour."

Great, flipping great! Here I was, wandering off into uncharted territory, facing a foe that may or may not shoot me before I even spoke a word. And all the while, these three were having food fantasies. Glad to see we were all on the same page.

I rose, grabbing a large, empty backpack that I hoped to fill in the next few hours.

"Okay, two hours there, two hours back," I said, playing with the broken zipper on the blue vinyl carrier. "As long as I don't get shot or something…" I gave my group a grin, "…I should be back by late afternoon."

They wished me their good lucks and patted me on the back. Then I began my journey into the unknown…again.

The walk went by quickly. Stepping off the gravel on the dead end just past Dizzy's place, I followed a trail of some kind along the edge of a large boggy swamp. While I had hunted back here a few times, it was always with Dizzy in the lead, hence my hesitation.

Keeping to the high (thus dry) side of the swamp, I wove between bare tree branches and patches of thorny brown berry brush. The crunching soil beneath my feet told me I'd return with dry shoes, which made me happy. The brush tearing at my pants reminded me to tread lightly and not toss it aside with my hand, which would leave me bloody and unhappy.

Pausing with the sun directly overhead, I spied fencing ahead. It was the tall kind meant to keep deer and other animals out...and perhaps people. It looked to me like the fencing stretched two hundred yards on the side closest to me. Another fence about the same length ran dead away from me, eastwards. Maybe 10 acres, I figured. Perhaps a little more.

I crept through the brush, hoping to approach unnoticed. At the very least, I wanted to give the appearance of being a reasonable, non-harm-intending man. That lasted all of about 50 steps.

"Come out of the brush with your hands held high where I can see them," a loud voice called out. "I've got you in my sight, and if I don't see those hands of yours within three seconds, I'm pulling the trigger."

I slowly raised my hands. So much for my stealthy approach.

Day 1,002 - continued

The man with the stainless steel rifle pointed at me was tall, thin and completely bald. I thought instantly of Ichabod Crane for some reason, though I couldn't recall if Crane was bald or not.

"Mr. Wilson?" I shouted, inching towards the wrong end of a barrel. "I'm not here for any trouble. I just need to talk."

Within 10 paces of one another, I saw his head raise from the wooden stock of the weapon. "Since you know who I am," he said, not sounding any nicer, "how about you tell me who you might be?"

I stopped and made sure to keep my hands where he could see them. "Bob Reiniger," I answered, hoping to see some sign of recognition in his face upon hearing the name. Suddenly it dawned on me: what if he and my grandpa had never met, or worse, didn't like one another?

"I knew your grandpa," he answered. He didn't sound upset, but the gun was still pointed at me. "What do you want?" Geez, he was all kinds of friendly.

Daringly, I stepped forward right up to the fence. "I need to talk to you. Lettie Hamshire sent me."

That got a smile. And the name caused the gun to lower, a little. "So you're that young fellow hanging out with Lettie and all her people. You changed locations…after the fire?"

I nodded, finally feeling safe. "We all had to move into my place. It's kind of cramped, but at least we're safe.

He seemed to approve, lowering the gunstock to the ground.

"Fire kill anyone?" he asked, sounding as if he didn't care one way or the other.

"Dizzy," I answered solemnly. "But he was shot. That gang of thieves tearing around on horseback caused it all."

He spit next to himself and nodded. "Clyde Barster and his gang of assholes," he muttered in disdain. "Not bad enough we all gotta live like this, but we gotta put up with the likes of him."

I leaned against the fence. "You know the guy?"

He shrugged, making brief eye contact. "I know everyone up here," he stated. It didn't sound like he was bragging, more like just something he knew. "He comes from down by Amasa. Robbed that place blind during the first winter. Now he stays alive by stealing from others. Poor Dizzy."

He extended a long-fingered hand through the fencing. "Thaddeus Wilson," he said, introducing himself.

I shook it, breathing a sigh of relief with the progress I was making, though I still had a long way to go with this one. "You can just call me Wilson, for obvious reasons," he continued. His eyes narrowed as he wet his lips. "I suppose you want to talk some rubbish about a pregnant girl now?"

Crap! This guy was prepared for anything. Next, he'd be guessing how many eggs I planned on fitting in my backpack.

He frowned, leaning on the opposite side of the fence. "It ain't ours, ya know." Oh, so he wanted to play it that way — denial. I already had the trump card for that angle.

"Tell me, Mr. Wilson," I began, fighting back a grin, "back when you had hair, what color was it?"

His face remained unchanged. "Can't really recall. Been a while since I lost it all."

"How about your ex-wife's? Or your boys?" I knew if I stayed after it, the truth would eventually pop. Plus, I already knew the answer.

"Don't see where that's none of your business," he answered, avoiding eye contact at all costs.

Time for the kill shot. "If I was a bettin' man, I'd say it was red. Somewhere there's red hair, right?" I rolled my head to force him to look me in the face.

He was quiet for several minutes, rubbing at his lips with

dirty fingers. "It was Jimmy," he finally surrendered in a quiet tone. "Johnny told me all about it. Said they were only intimate once, not that it matters now, I suppose."

"And she has arrived," I added, noting the surprise in his face.

"She?" he asked, his voice catching on the single word.

"Yes," I replied, nodding. "A beautiful little girl named Hope."

I saw the corners of his lips curl slightly. "Seems like a funny name, given what we're up against nowadays."

I smiled and nodded. I agreed, but funny as it sounded, Hope was the only thing keeping us from giving up.

Day 1,003

I returned from my adventure with a bounty none of us could've ever imagined. With the weight of my bag and an extra gunnysack thrust upon me by Wilson, I didn't return until well after dark. It wasn't until I flopped the bags onto the floor and myself on the couch that things began to add up.

My strange new friend left me standing by his fence for several hours as he assembled a care package. He mentioned something about it being 'his duty'. Couldn't have a poor defenseless baby starve to death, he claimed, not as long as he could help.

So I waited, sitting against the fence, while the white, puffy clouds occasionally blocked the direct sunlight, only to race eastward after a bit. Behind me, the sounds of cows and sheep droned into the warm spring afternoon.

I had fallen asleep by the time he came back. Guiding me to a gate in the mid-section of his fencing, he undid the lock and passed the hefty sack to me.

"I'd like to come visit sometime, if I could," he requested.

We agreed on several days from then and parted ways with another handshake.

He never told me what was in the bag, but Lettie, Marge and Daisy tore into it as soon as I dropped it to the floor.

Inside was a cornucopia of goods that took our breath away. Wilson, it seemed, was a resourceful man in the wilderness.

Marge and Daisy announced each gift: three cans of powdered lemonade, two dozen carefully packed eggs, a package wrapped in white butcher paper with a large pile of smoked ham, six small containers of milk and a small bag of flour.

Daisy began to cry when she reached the bottom of the sack.

"Containers..." she gasped, brushing way tears. "Four containers of powdered baby formula."

How and why raced through my mind. Somehow in the middle of the worst the world could throw at us, this tall, thin, rather dull-looking man had the answer to all of our prayers.

Hope sucked formula from the bottle, only stopping to be burped midway through. It was then I realized that the baby had cried very little. Finally, we were all able to sleep and breathe like normal people again.

When Hope finished the second bottle, Daisy burped her

and laid the happy child on some blankets on the couch. Her cooing lulled her to sleep almost instantly.

Beside me, Lettie stared at the miracle.

"Never thought that child would quit screaming," she crowed, peeking over the edge of the blankets at her. "Glad her mother is finally happy as well. She getting dressed?"

She addressed the last part to Marge, or perhaps Daisy. I had no idea what the teen mother was up to.

"She said she wanted to look nice for Mr. Wilson's visit," Daisy answered, scurrying about the room. "Has anyone seen the hairbrush?"

While we only had one hairbrush, that wasn't the worst of it. Seven people also shared two toothbrushes. And all toothpaste had vanished with the fire at Lettie's home.

"He said he'd come sometime after high noon," I announced, pondering whether I should head outside and cut some more wood. Remembering that it might wake Hope, I decided to hold off. Instead, I sat on the bench out front to keep an eye on Nate and Libby.

Though not as warm as the previous week, the sun still felt good. Everything felt good, actually. We finally had a little food, a happy baby and the pressure of the daily grind had loosened, thanks to Wilson's promise of sharing what he could.

Deep inside, the reality of my world darkened my soul. There was a problem that needed solving, and soon, before it found us again.

Lettie must have seen it on my face when she joined me outside.

"You know, everyone is well aware of what bothers you." It wasn't really a question, more of a statement from the old woman.

I nodded minutely. "It's not going away, you know. When I went for the last of the food after your place burned down, there were strange tracks by the cellar door. Not mine for sure. And three or four sets of them. They know we had more."

Lettie huffed at my wisdom. "Well, they ought to know it's all gone by now then."

That made sense, but the idea of those people attacking one last time, even if we prevailed, made my stomach flip.

"It's only a matter of time before they show up here, Lettie," I replied quietly. "I know it, you know it…" I thrust a thumb over my shoulder. "And they all know it. Gotta be dealt with."

Gently, she patted my hands. "Just give it a little more time," she said. "Just a little more. Then you can do what you got to."

Day 1,006

I must have had my days mixed up. Or heard wrong. It wasn't until almost a full week after my initial visit with Wilson that I saw him walking down the road in a slight drizzle.

From a fog he appeared, dressed in an old black suit coat, matching pants that were a bit too short and what looked like a fresh white shirt. Behind him he pulled a wagon. The clanging metal wheels announced his arrival as he descended from the roadway.

"Thaddeus Wilson," Lettie announced from the doorway. "I haven't laid eyes on you since before this hell all began."

He tipped the wide-brimmed black hat in her direction. "Afternoon, Lettie." He nodded at me. "Bob." From the way he was dressed he could have once upon a time been mistaken for Amish or Mennonite. Now he was just another odd character in our equally odd world.

"What'd you bring us, Wilson?" I asked, pointing at his wagon.

Removing his hat, he ran a hand over his smooth head. "Oh, just a couple more things," he drawled, looking at the wagon more than Lettie or I. "Just some stuff I didn't need that I thought you could use."

"Some beef jerky, dried and salted bacon, half-dozen large jars of boiled potatoes." He walked back and lifted the tarp. "Some dried beets, turnips, grapes." He lifted a bag and tossed it at us. "And this was the bonus find."

I opened it, unsure of what I might find. Pieces of white cloth. I pulled one out and held it up for Lettie's inspection. She smiled.

"Cloth diapers," she proclaimed. "Those will come in mighty handy." She cast a glance at our visitor. "Where'd you come up with them, Thaddeus?"

He grinned youthfully. "Me and the wife never threw anything out. Never knew when you might be able to use it."

I nodded, understanding the wisdom. "Where'd you get the baby formula?" I asked. "I would think all the canned stuff would have been long gone by now."

Playing with his hat, he shrugged. "I'm a good trader," he stated modestly. "People want what I got, food mostly. I knew that little girl was coming before last winter. So I put the word out."

He stared at me seriously. "Got to protect our own," he said, his eyes never leaving mine. "And I got news for you on Barster's location. But first, I'd like to see my granddaughter, if you don't mind."

Ah, quid pro quo. I could produce a baby. Especially if it meant I received the information I so desperately needed. Together, we all went inside.

Violet shook as she met her father-in-law, per se. In all actuality, Wilson was just Hope's grandfather, but the teen, who had no intensions of marrying Jimmy Wilson, still put on all the faces of a girl at her first dance.

Tears formed in the man's eyes as he peered at the child, sleeping in her mother's arms. When asked if he wanted to hold her, he shook his head.

"Never held a little girl before," he said in a quiet, almost embarrassed tone. "Wouldn't want to break her."

Daisy stepped forward and took Hope in her arms. "Just put your arms out. I'll help you," she said, her loving voice causing the man to nod slightly. "I'm sure Vi would love to have you hold her."

Holding the baby stiff-armed, he tipped his head forward and kissed her forehead. Almost as quickly as she was nestled in his thin arms, he handed her back to Daisy.

"Better take her," he said, sniffing back tears. "I'm about to explode with joy, and I don't want to blubber all over this precious gift."

I didn't know what I had expected, but this wasn't it. For all appearances, Thaddeus Wilson was perhaps the most stoic man I'd ever met. Watching him take a handkerchief from his back pocket and blow his nose, then dry his eyes, I too was moved with emotion.

"We have some needs we should talk about," he continued, turning to Lettie and me.

Yes, yes we did. My revenge for Dizzy's death was still my main priority. Luck would have it that this man held the information I badly wanted to hear.

Day 1,006 - continued

Outside in the shade, Wilson, Lettie, Marge and I took spots on the bench and chairs. Wilson's face had returned to its normal state, tight and dour. He nodded to the women.

"First thing we need to obtain are some staples," he began in his baritone voice. "I don't know how you are on flour and salt, but I'm damn near out."

"Same here," Lettie answered, nodding as she spoke. "Little sugar wouldn't hurt either."

"There's a fish camp up in Ontonagon that is supposed to have plenty of dry goods like we're looking for," Wilson reported, twirling his hat in his hands. "I've got some dried meat I can send, but rumor has it what they really need is people." He glanced up at us all.

I peeked at Lettie while she stared at Marge. Marge's blue eyes were fixed on Wilson.

"Got a body you can spare for six months?" Wilson asked. "They'll pay that person's body weight in supplies. I'll have Johnny go up with a cart full of my stuff. Whoever can walk with him. It's about 75 miles. Three days up and three days back. What do you think, Bob?"

Not me, I thought. I didn't want to waste another day, much less a week, in going after Dizzy's murderers. However, I noticed all eyes were focused my direction.

"He can't go," Lettie stated plainly. "He's our protection. What about your boy, Marge?"

She shook her head violently like it was the worst idea she'd ever heard.

"Someone needs to go," Wilson continued. "It's only six months. Be over quicker than you think. And you'd be back by the time the snows got real bad."

Our group sat silent for several minutes, each of us contemplating new supplies and what that would mean for the others…and six months away from home.

"I'll go," Marge replied, barely above a whisper.

That set me sideways for a moment. "Are you sure, Marge?"

She nodded. "I'm healthy; Daisy can help take care of Violet and the baby. She has more recent firsthand experience than I do. Nate can get along without me for that long, I'm sure."

Wilson cleared his throat. "Speaking of your boy, I was wondering if he'd maybe come and live with me and mine for the summer. We can really use the extra help now that we're planting and tending to crops. Probably do him some good as far as growing up concerns."

Against what I believed to be astronomical odds, I saw Marge peek at Lettie and nod.

"Yes," Marge replied. "That would be good for him I believe."

I slid forward on the bench, reaching for her hands and attention. "Are you sure about this, Marge? Not just Nate, but yourself as well?"

She looked at me, fierce determination flashing in her eyes. "We all have to do whatever it takes to survive, Bob. So yes, I'm sure of everything."

She may have been certain, but I wondered how Violet would take the news, giving up her mother and her brother for the upcoming summer.

Day 1,009

Marge left with Johnny Wilson, disappearing in a thick shroud of fog. They strolled north on the blacktop, heading for Covington. From there, they would turn northwest towards Ontonagon, another 65 miles plus.

To the south, we watched as Nate and Wilson vanished. He had some sort of secret route he took to his place. I always headed down Dizzy Drive to get back there. Lettie tried to explain it to me, but it was confusing. I just accepted the fact that a man who had lived in No Where all of his life knew his way around.

Daisy stood next to me, rocking little Hope back to sleep after one of her two morning bottles. Tears streaked her pale cheeks, dripping freely to the floor.

"How's Violet taking all of this, now that D-Day is here?" I asked in a hushed tone.

Daisy shrugged, readjusting the squirming child in her arms.

"She and Marge aren't really all that close," she replied, turning to check the room. I did the same. Only Lettie was there, snoozing in her typical spot. Violet was absent, most likely changing in the bedroom since the door was closed.

"And Marge has always been closer to Nate," Daisy continued. "I don't think Vi is going to miss them half as much as if you had left."

I rolled my eyes and headed outside to cut some wood. Daisy had a theory, and a stupid one at that. Secretly, she felt Violet adored me. That went against our entire relationship in my mind.

Whenever the teen spoke to me, a fair amount of disdain colored her tone. Sure, she stayed with me both times after I was shot, but her 'oh-look-what-you've-done-to-yourself-now' attitude made any sort of covert infatuation sound crazy to me. Holding the ax in my hands, I pondered the next few months. Wilson gave me directions to three probable locations for the Barster gang. According to recent reports, they were down to three people, though they were still on the attack. The two men he knew who were still living possessed alleged nasty dispositions, according to Wilson. And that was before the end of the world as we knew it.

By verbal agreement and a firm handshake, I promised Wilson I wouldn't attack until the supplies were back and delivered by him. Only then would I leave and he would take my place on guard, watching over my family.

"Reduced family," I said aloud, staring at the ax blade.

"What's a reduced family?" A small voice asked from behind me, which made me nearly crap my pants. Turning, I spied Libby on a stump by the south end of the cabin. Her bare feet swung back and forth in a childish motion. Ants in her pants, Lettie claimed.

"We just have less, that's all," I replied, trying to gauge her mood. Normally she was a happy child. Now, I could tell by her frown she wasn't feeling the same. ""What's wrong, Libby?"

"I didn't want Nate to go," she whined softly. "He played with me a lot. Who's going to play with me now?"

"I will," a new voice answered. I looked up to see Violet coming through the door. If she were trying to cheer the little girl's spirit, perhaps a smile would have helped.

"Lettie says we need to turn that dirt again in the garden," Violet said to me, pointing just short of the road. "Since Daisy helped you last week, I figured I'd give her a break and help out today."

I grabbed the shovels while Violet and Libby played a quick game of tag. Standing in the spayed dirt, I watched Violet grab her shovel and start to turn in the far corner. Libby mimicked her with a stick.

"Can I ask you a question?" I asked, thinking she might turn when I spoke, but she didn't. "Violet, can I ask you a question?"

She spun and scowled at me. "No, I won't miss her, or either of them," she spewed. "My mother told me she hated me when she found out I was pregnant. She turned Nate against me too. If Daisy hadn't shown up, I don't know how I'd still be alive." She went back to her shoveling. "So quit being so damn nosey and sentimental and dig. I don't want to be out here all day."

Chuckling to myself, I put my back into the work. So much for Daisy and her wild theories.

Day 1,012

The two-day rain finally abated with a warm, late spring morning. It was a good thing the skies turned off the spigot. Lettie was all over me about planting, something I knew absolutely nothing about.

We spent the morning and well into the afternoon in the garden, "we" being Violet, Daisy and I. The other "we's", Lettie and Libby, sat on an old lawn chair in the shade some 20 yards away. The old woman went between helping Libby with her spelling and barking orders at her manual labor crew.

My lack of experience tripled when it came to my crew. Daisy knew less than I did about gardens, Violet a little more than that. If you can count picking beans and other vegetables for two years at Lettie's, we all had some experience. I wanted to appoint Violet as foreperson, but Daisy warned me her mood was no better than it had been for the past few days sans mother.

"I think the baby's crying again," Libby reported, strolling towards the cabin door. "I'll get her and bring her out."

"No," instantly shot from my lips. No way could a five-year-old handle a squirming infant in my mind.

"Just be careful, sweetie," Daisy called out, looking up at me with her hands placed solidly on her hips. "She can do it just fine."

I raised my hands in mock surrender with a smile. "Hey, if it's okay with Violet, it's fine with me. All I was saying—"

"You know," Violet snarled, removing her gloves and tossing them in the sandy dirt, "you're about the only one who doesn't pick the baby up, Bob." Her glare intensified as she drew nearer. "You got something against babies?"

Three sets of eyes zeroed in on me. For a moment, I felt like a condemned person.

"It's just with all you women here—"

Violet stepped closer. "Oh, so babies are women's work only?"

Lettie was laughing, Daisy grinning. *Thanks for the help ladies,* I thought bitterly.

"It's not my child, Violet," I answered, going back to planting golden sweet corn seeds.

Now she stood above me, her shadow covering my sun. "You're really an asshole, you know that, Bob?"

I looked up at her. "I got things I gotta do, little girl. Adult things. You take care of your child and I'll take care of the more dangerous stuff."

I noticed Daisy next to her, stroking her arm.

"Are you going to try and come back in one piece this time?" Violet vented. "Or are you going to do something stupid and get killed?"

"Vi, that's enough," Daisy said in a soft but firm tone. "Leave it be."

She turned on her friend hastily. "You've never had to fix him up," Violet ranted. "You've never seen the blood pouring out of his body. You've never been so scared in all your life that someone was gonna die right in front of you."

She glared down at me again, tears welling in her eyes. "You don't need to do this, Bob," Violet added. "You can wait for them. Kill them when they show up here. You don't need to avenge Dizzy — not if it means getting yourself killed. He wouldn't want it that way!"

I rose, towering over the pair. Both wept openly. "I can't risk them coming and hurting any of you. Not here. I couldn't live with myself."

Violet lashed at my chest with her bare hands. "If you don't live, I don't want to live," she cried. Turning, she noticed Libby approaching with Hope in her arms. "It's not fair to her; it's not fair to me, to Daisy, to Libby, or even to Lettie. We need you alive."

She took one last swing and I grabbed her arm. "Well, you'd all better pray I get the job done then. Because I'm not backing down from it, not this time. It ends when Wilson comes back."

She pushed away. "You make me so mad, Bob Reiniger!" she shrieked. "So damn mad!"

I watched as Violet turned Libby back towards the house. Daisy chased after them as Lettie laughed at the circus from her chair.

"Guess it's just you and me, young man." I heard Lettie rise from the chair. "Come on, I'll help."

I watched the quartet disappear into the cabin. "What was all that about?" I asked, opening a new bag of seeds.

"Just people who care, that's all," she answered. "We know you got to take care of it. Just don't expect any of us to send you off to war with our blessings."

"Tough shit," I whispered. I was going, and if I had to die trying to exact revenge, then so be it. They'd all be fine without me.

Day 1,014

I crept through the woods, stopping and kneeling often. Stealthily, I checked my target. Damn it, her hand was up again.

"I heard you again," Libby called out, turning the page of the book on her lap. "You aren't very good at this." Dressed down by a child. That hurt.

My shoulders slumped as I let out a long sigh. "I'm going back a couple more yards to start again," I replied from the edge of the woods. She nodded while I turned and started back.

"Try being quieter," she yelled. "Like a mouse, *not* a moose." I heard her laugh to herself as I tromped deeper into the budding foliage. Another few weeks and everything would be in near summer splendor.

I didn't have two weeks. In my mind, I didn't want to wait another two *days* for the goods to be delivered. I was anxious to get at the deed while my heart was still in it.

"I'll show her a mouse," I muttered, dodging bare tree branches.

Stopping, I turned back towards the cabin. "Call out the

minute you hear me this time, Libby. Don't just raise your hand...yell it out. Okay?"

"Okay," she sassed back. Good, I'd show her this time.

The entire purpose of this exercise was to get me close to my targets without the chance of them hearing me. I'd assumed the damp spring brush and carpet of leaves would hide my movements. Lettie suggested a trial run, using someone with good ears and not someone who doted on a screaming baby all of the time.

Libby won, whether she liked it or not. Since she was happy and not complaining, I was learning a lot.

I changed my game plan and sneaked forward in a new direction, more at the back end of the cabin than my previous attempts. The little turd would be listening for me coming straight at her. Now we'd find out if I could sneak like a mouse.

One step, two steps, three steps. I paused. *So far so good*, I thought. No word from my target...yet. Another two steps and a small piece of brush cracked under my left foot. *Damn it*, I scolded myself. She had to have heard that.

Kneeling again, I waited for her to call me out. Nothing. Good. I was getting better with each trail run. Finally on this fifth try, I was making progress.

Another dozen carefully placed steps and I spied the back end of the cottage. It was yards away, and still no word from Libby of being discovered. I was ready, I just needed to crawl out of the woods and slither around the far end of the place. This time, I'd scare the living crap out of her.

Safely out of the woods, I dashed to the north side of the structure. Still, nothing from my spotter. I rested against the cool logs, deeply breathing in their musty odor. *Maybe I should treat the wood,* I wondered, but the thought passed quickly as I refocused on the task at hand.

Standing on my tiptoes, I inched my way to the front, hugging the logs. I paused and could hear Daisy speaking, but not Libby. Maybe her mother had distracted her. That was okay, I figured. There would be distractions with the Barster gang.

Peeking around the corner, I spied Daisy. She was wringing her small hands together and pleading with someone, perhaps Lettie or Violet?

"You don't need to do this," she said, her voice soft but nervous. "We can give you what you want."

That didn't make any sense. She must be talking to Violet. What was that damn un-agreeable teen up to now?

I gave myself up and rounded the corner. It was only then

that I saw them all.

Daisy, Libby and a strange man wielding a knife, the sharp tip held against Libby's throat.

Playtime was over.

Day 1,014 - continued

Slowly I raised my hands above my head, palms open towards the scene and the man with the knife.

"Let's take it easy here, friend," I managed calmly, inching toward a shaking Daisy. "No one needs to get hurt. Just tell us what you want and we'll take care of it."

His threatening dirty grin shook me to the core. "Yeah, play nice and no one will get hurt," he replied in a gravelly tone, "especially this sweet little girl here."

He stayed behind her, the knife held firmly to Libby's throat. "Have someone fetch me a big old plate of food," he continued, licking his lips. "And fill me up a bag of goodies for when I leave."

He waved the knife at Daisy and me. "Why don't you turn around nice and slow like, buddy. Let me see if you got a weapon on you."

I did as requested, knowing my 45 was exposed on my belt behind me.

"Give that gun to that pretty little mother there," he continued. "And have her hand it to me."

We did as ordered. Daisy's hands shook as she gave the gun

to the intruder.

"Please don't hurt my daughter," she begged. "Please."

His grin broadened as he studied Daisy. "I ain't gonna hurt her. Not if I get what I want, sweetie pie."

Daisy moved back beside me, wrapping her arms around my waist.

I felt Daisy trembling. Nodding my understanding, I moved slowly for the front door. When I turned to open it, Violet stood on the other side with the plate of requested food. She stared at me stone-faced.

"I'll give it to him," I whispered.

Violet stared past me and flinched. "I'll take care of it," she replied, pushing her way outside.

When I turned, I noticed the man putting something around Libby's quivering throat. She wasn't weeping yet, but her cheeks were streaked with tears.

"This little necklace is going to keep us all honest," the stranger continued, snapping it shut behind her head. "If you give me what I want, I'll release it from her, down the road a little bit. If you try anything funny…well, you won't be able to take it off without killing her."

I studied the maniacal device. Two dark strands of thin wire ran parallel around Libby's neck. Every two inches or so, two thicker pieces of wire stuck up. It looked like something modified from a small-game trap. The wires that stuck up from the device made my stomach flip nervously.

"If you try to take this off," the man continued, rising from behind Libby, "it's gonna spring these wires. And they're going to shoot into this little sweetie's neck. And then you're gonna have a bloody mess on your hands."

Daisy wept beside me; Violet shook uncontrollably next to her. Lettie must have still been inside, watching Hope. We had a problem, and as far as I could tell, the only solution was to give this drifter what he wanted. No matter how badly it set us back.

He nodded at Violet and the plate of food. "I think I'll eat now." He motioned at Daisy and me with his free hand, the other still holding the knife close to Libby. "You two go fill me a big ol' bag with more food. This young woman can keep me company while I eat."

I started to reply, but Violet shot me a look. "Do what he wants," she said calmly. "Let's get this over with."

I watched as she led Libby to the bench and sat her down. Studying the necklace, Violet spoke softly to the young child in a comforting tone, "Now, you just stay here and we'll have that off of you in no time. Don't play with it."

"Come here, young lady," the man called out, holding up a spoonful of stew. "You take the first bite so I know this ain't poisoned."

Violet did as asked, wiping some of the slop from her chin when he tried to feed her too large a spoonful. I noticed his eyes wandering about on her body. For a moment, I considered charging him and pummeling him into the dirt. But the necklace warned me not to.

His dirty hands slid over Violet's hips; I saw her blanch. Recovering quickly, she pointed away from the cabin. "Not here," she said aloud as I followed Daisy inside. "We need to do this away from the girl, okay?"

Again, I wanted to charge him but something told me Violet was just doing what she had to, all to protect Libby.

The two stopped near the road. I stared through the front window, watching as Violet laughed and turned away slightly. When he reached for her breasts, she playfully slapped away his approach. More giggling followed and I became stupefied.

"What the hell is she doing?" I asked. Behind me, I could hear Daisy digging through the cupboards.

"She knows what she needs to do," Daisy replied. "She'll keep him at bay."

Again, he pulled Violet in close, attempting to kiss her neck.

She resisted, but not enough for my liking. His hand rose on her back, pulling her near, causing my stomach to twist. When that same hand slid down to her rear and patted it, then squeezed, I lost my patience.

"Give me that damn bag," I shouted, turning to face Daisy. "I gotta get out there before this gets any worse. She doesn't need to go this far."

I grabbed the bag from Daisy's outstretched hand, only for her to drop it before I could get a good hold.

Her sharp inhale and hands shooting to her mouth caused me to spin.

That's when I saw the attack.

Day 1,014 - continued

I hadn't seen the initial plunge, the one that caught Daisy off guard. However, I did witness the next two. And they were as brutal as anything I'd ever done myself.

The plate was in mid-air when I turned around, the man's hands now off Violet's body, clutching at his midsection.

Her arm twisted behind again, and I saw the glint of sun gleam off of the steel blade. A second time, or perhaps already a third, Violet thrust the blade into a free spot that wasn't guarded by his hands. The drifter fell forward to his knees, his hands searching for the weapon. But it was in vain; the damage was done.

With another blow, Violet plunged the blade just below his left shoulder as I sprinted from the cabin towards the melee. Pulling it out, she leaned in for one last cut - the kill shot to his throat.

By the time I got to her, she was kicking the nearly dead form, screaming obscenities.

"It's over," I shouted, wrapping my arms around the seething teen. Still she pushed at him. "Violet, he's dead. It's done."

She loosened in my arms, dropping the large pocket knife to the dirt. Leaning past me, she spit at him. "Piece of rotten, no good, slimy shit," she spewed.

I held her for a few moments more, making sure he was dead. The gurgling from the bloody froth coming from his neck ceased, as the last semblances of life did as well. Only then did Violet nod and look up at me.

"We need to drag him across the road so your wild pets can have him for dinner," she said, her words scarily calm for someone who'd just killed a guy.

She glanced back at the cabin, frowning for a moment. "I hope Libby wasn't looking when I stabbed him," she added, pushing away from my embrace. "Ah, whatever. She needs to learn how to survive."

She grabbed one of the drifter's lifeless arms and stared up at me. "Are you gonna help me? Or are you going to make me do this all by myself? I'm just a girl, ya know."

I felt my head moving from side to side. Though she had solved one problem, a bigger one still loomed.

"What are we going to do with that device around Libby's throat?" I asked, grabbing the loose arm. "You didn't think this through, Violet. We got a real problem."

Dragging the corpse over the road, she laughed at me. "Oh

ye of little faith," she responded. "That's not a problem," she shrugged, "not much of one."

Given the sobbing I could hear from inside the cabin, Violet was sadly mistaken. We had a huge problem, and the only one who could solve it was dead at our feet.

Back inside the cabin, I crouched next to Libby. While she was attempting to be brave, her tears suggested otherwise.

I inspected the device, not liking what I found. It was already tight, far too tight to flip over and render harmless. Furthermore, I could see the tension in the springs, ready to snap at the first wrong move.

"You have to get that off of her," Daisy whined into my ear. "Please, Bob. Get it off."

I turned and smiled at the terrified mother. "I'm working on it. Just need to figure it out. Don't want it going off and hurting Libby."

Lettie leaned in, studying the device. "Those prongs look like they're off a squirrel or opossum trap of some kind," she said. "If they can kill a varmint…"

Yeah, thanks, Lettie. No sense in sugarcoating an already dire situation, I thought. Beside me, Daisy's crying intensified.

"Maybe we can put pieces of wood under each jaw, and

work on it that way," I suggested. No one dared offer their opinion, so I thought aloud. "Or maybe we can bend them back. That way when they go off they won't dig into her skin…too badly."

"And what happens when they snap while you're playing with them?" Daisy asked in an appropriately tense tone.

I shrugged, mostly to myself. "Yeah, there's that possibility."

Violet pushed her way in close, touching the jaws with her fingers. She used a much less delicate touch than I had.

Straightening next to me, she crossed her arms. "It's a ruse," she stated. "From what I see, it won't go off."

For all it was worth, she sounded confident. But I sure didn't feel that brave.

"I say we try the wood option," I suggested, searching the room for agreement. Still, my housemates didn't look convinced.

Pushing me aside again, Violet leaned in closer. "Cut the tips off," she stated. "Then we can do whatever we want with the rest of it. But I'm still betting the thing won't trip."

Lettie placed a hand on my shoulder. "You got a wire nippers?" I nodded. "Then I agree. Cut the tips off that damn contraption. That way it will just pinch if it goes off."

Beside me, Daisy sucked in a short breath, her face filled

with horror.

"Little pinch ain't gonna kill her," Lettie added, rubbing Daisy's shoulder.

I waited for Daisy to decide; it was her child who was potentially in harm's way after all. Finally, after a long, silent deliberation, she nodded her agreement.

"I'll get the nippers," I said, heading for the pantry.

"It's not going off," Violet replied in one of her snotty tones. I saw her smile at Daisy, uneasy. "At least I don't think it will."

Great. Now I was taking Libby's life in my hands on the advice of an *almost*-certain teen. Wonderful.

Day 1,014 - continued

Carefully, I applied pressure to the nipper handles. But the wire refused to cut. Moving it further into the jaws of the tool only made my group suck in their breaths collectively. Some help they were.

"Put a little of that lack of muscle into it," Violet whispered into my ear. "At this rate, she'll choke to death."

"Not helping," I mumbled, making sure Lettie and Daisy were out of earshot. "You got any other bright ideas?"

Daisy occupied her time by bouncing Hope on her hip, only nervously peeking at Violet and me every other second or so. *That's not helping!* I almost said aloud. But the terror in her eyes made me refocus.

"It's not going to snap," Violet repeated for the umpteenth time. Reaching forward, she played with the device. "Are there even springs in this thing?"

I popped up and led her out of the cabin. "Be right back," I called to Lettie and Daisy, who were staring google-eyed at us. "Just need to discuss an idea."

Outside, Violet chased away one of the first flies of summer. "It's not real," she snapped. "Just pull it off her neck and this will all be over."

I stared down into her eyes. "Are you willing to risk Libby's life on your hunch? In case you didn't notice, Daisy is almost at her wit's end."

She pushed me away. "Then quit horsing around and cut those prongs, okay?" Scrunching her nose at me, I saw doubt in her eyes.

"You're not sure, are you?" I asked.

She shook her head. "I was just acting brave for Daisy and Libby's sake."

Good God; of all the trouble she'd caused me before, this took the cake.

"Maybe you killed him just a little too quickly, aye?"

A scowl crossed her face. "He was a pig and a freeloader. He was going to steal all of our food. Someone needed to kill him."

I leaned in closer. "I was going to wait until Libby was safe, in case you were wondering."

The door cracked open behind me. We both turned to find Lettie staring at us.

"You two want to come back in here and get this contraption off Libby?" she asked, shaking her head at us. "Mother and daughter are getting a little anxious. You two can argue about whatever you're yapping about later."

"Cut the tips," Violet seethed, pounding her fist into my shoulder.

Lettie placed a hand on my chest as I tried to walk past her. "Everything okay there, Bob?" Her expression told me she wanted the truth.

I paused and thought for a moment. "Just a little difference of opinion on what exactly we're doing, that's all. Got it cleared up now."

She nodded before taking her hand away. "Good. Because you're going to have to figure out what to do for Daisy's heart attack if you don't take care of this soon. Hustle up."

Another great motivational speech from the senior member of our group. Just the kind and caring words of inspiration I needed.

A few minutes passed before I tossed the wire nippers aside. They wouldn't cut the steel prongs. I needed something else, something more robust.

Lettie dug out our meager toolbox. "Screwdriver, Phillips screwdriver, monkey wrench, Allen keys." She listed the contents as if reading an old recipe card. "Got a file, maybe that will work?"

Libby wiggled with boredom. Daisy paced with anxiety. I squeezed my eyes tightly shut, wondering what to do next.

"Bingo!" Lettie shouted. "Pliers. These should work."

She handed them to me with a large smile. But I didn't see their usefulness. Were we going to *pull* the prongs away?

"And these help how?" I asked, trying to sound less skeptical than I felt.

She pointed at the tool. "The jaws, near the hinge. You can cut with those."

I gave her a look and thought, *No way old lady.*

"I've done it before," she continued. I expected her to sound irritated. Instead, she sounded damn near like a braggart. "Just get them in there as close as you can and nip the wires. Should work." She nodded, as if to boost my confidence.

Carefully, I used her described technique on the first wire. Much to my surprise, it worked. But there was a problem. One short piece of metal remained intact.

"Don't worry about that," Lettie scolded as I poked at it. "Just keep cutting. The worst it can do is pinch her a little."

Whether Daisy shrieked at the idea or Lettie's callous explanation, I wasn't sure. I went back to work.

In a few short minutes, all of the prongs were gone, six sets of short wires left that may or may not pinch Libby when removing the device. For the last part of the procedure, I turned to Violet.

"Okay," I said, letting her take my place next to Libby, "do what you got to do. But be careful."

Taking a seat, Violet shook her head at me. "Be careful," she mocked in a childish tone. "Like I'd be anything else."

Easing the nippers under one of the two metals strands, she peered around at Libby's anxious face. "Nothing's going to happen, sweetie. This will all be over in a minute or two."

Libby nodded, wiping her dripping nose with the butt of her palm.

Daisy leaned close. "Are you sure this is okay, Vi?" she whispered.

The teen simply nodded and went back to work.

Snap!

Our group jumped. Daisy screamed, assuming the worst. Violet turned and glared at all of us.

"It was just me cutting the wire," she seethed, again shaking her head. "Now if you'd all be quiet and show a little more confidence, I'll get this taken care of."

The second wired gave way with the same snap as the first, and Violet proudly held the necklace up for our inspection.

"See, it never even went off. I told you it was a ruse."

We all sighed a breath of relief. Daisy snatched Libby from her stool and kissed her over and over again. Rising from her spot, Violet gave me a smirk and thrust the device out in front of her.

Lettie gingerly took the necklace, examining it with an uneasy caution, as if it might still bite. When she handed it to me, the whole thing exploded with a loud *snap!*

Violet shrugged, showing no guilt or embarrassment. "We got it off her," she snarked. "No big deal."

Yeah, whatever girly, I thought. *It could have been a deadly big deal.*

Day 1,016

Together, we established a new rule. No more repeats of "the Libby Incident", as we now referred to it. No longer would she be allowed outside unattended. If we were out, she could be as well. Under no circumstances was she to be by herself.

I now also carried my gun at all times, no exceptions. Planting the garden, gun on me. Going to the well, gun on me. A quick run to the outhouse, gun on me. No more roaming around with my gun lying on the counter inside.

As an added precaution, we kept Lettie's 30-30 loaded and propped next to the door. If anyone saw anything that made them uncomfortable, they were to grab the rifle and jack a shell into the chamber.

That was a safety measure I insisted upon, loading the gun. The old rifle held six shells in its below-barrel magazine. We wouldn't force one into the chamber until needed. If something happened and the gun tipped over, it couldn't go off that way. But having it at the ready, fully loaded, was essential. And everyone happily agreed to the plan.

Watching the afternoon rain roll off the roof and into large puddles, my frown deepened.

According to my calculations, Johnny Wilson had left eight days ago. Or maybe it was only seven. The point was, I had a plan in place for my attack. All I needed was for my family's safety net to show up so I could put it into action.

Three days up and three days back was what old man Wilson had claimed. That made his return a day or two late. Given the steady rain, I wondered if another day might pass before I got going.

I heard footsteps behind me as I gazed out the front window, then a hand on my arm. When I looked down at the small hand, I knew who it was: Daisy.

Ever since we had taken the maniacal torture device off of Libby's neck, Daisy had been quiet. I didn't think she was angry about anything, at least not something I had done. Perhaps Violet's youthful ignorance had upset her.

"No one back yet?" she asked, her tone soft, tinged with fear. "Maybe when the rain lets up. Mr. Wilson probably doesn't want to haul flour here in the rain." I felt her nod against my side, agreeing with her own logic. "That's probably best."

It wasn't what she said, it was what she refused to talk about. Particularly my leaving — my plan for revenge.

We took a spot on the couch and were promptly handed Hope. I gazed up at Lettie, the person who had offered us the infant.

"She needs her diaper changed and another bottle," Lettie announced, turning for the stove. "I'll get the bottle started if one of you wants to change her. Be sure to use that coconut oil on her bottom so that damn rash doesn't come back. I can't handle another night with a screaming baby."

For as much as we complained amongst ourselves, Hope was a happy baby. Given the fact she was born in a time that resembled the early 1800s, she was a great baby.

"What's her mother up to?" I asked as Daisy went about the chore at hand. "Haven't seen her much today. She still in bed?"

Not turning to reveal her expression, Lettie poured warm water from the stove into the one bottle we had. "She has a touch of the blues," she answered plainly. "Might be the weather. Might be postpartum. Could be something else. She and Libby are in the bedroom cuddling. Maybe that will help her feel better."

Oh great, this again, I thought.

I checked Daisy for a response. She didn't look away from Hope once as she cooed at the baby. Lettie still refused to make eye contact. Violet was in hiding. Like I didn't know what any of that meant.

"You know," I began, trying to control the anger in my voice, "I'm doing this for our protection. It's not like I'm running off to fight some mythical dragon. These people have proven they're a real threat."

I could've sworn I saw Lettie shrug at my words. When I peeked at Daisy, I noticed her nodding slightly. But still no words.

"We are discussing this tonight," I stated, rising from the couch. "When Hope and Libby are asleep, everyone is going to have their say. Then it's over. Got it?"

I only got two slight head nods and not a sound from the bedroom, which was good enough for me.

Day 1,016 - continued

Seated around the table, we silently stared at one another. Next to me was Daisy, on her right sat Violet. Lettie sat on my left, fighting a sock she was mending.

"Let's hear it," I stated, my eyes going between the trio of naysayers. "Time to get it all out in the open."

"We all know what you got to do," Lettie began frankly. "Just none of us are too excited to see you die."

I could always count on the old bird to get things started with her honest input. Instantly tears formed in Daisy's and Violet's eyes.

"I think it's stupid," Violet whimpered, wiping away tears. "Going after killers isn't the smartest thing." She glared at me. "They're killers after all. So...duh."

Taking my hands, Daisy tried to smile before speaking. She did not attempt to chase away any of her sorrow. "I don't want you to get hurt, and you know that. I just keep thinking there's another way to solve this, one we haven't thought of yet."

Much to their credit, no one held back. I wanted honesty, and that was exactly what they were giving me. Now it was my turn.

"Wilson gave me three locations they could be at," I began. Scratching the back of my neck, I craned my head to the left. "I'm going to start with the closest and work my way out. I'll creep in at night and hide in the thickest brush I can find. That way, come morning, I'll be able to watch what's going on without being seen."

Violet shot me a nasty look. "And if they see you sneaking in? If they catch you before you hide. What then?" she objected.

I opened my mouth to reply, but she cut me off. "They'll kill you, that's what. And when they come here, whether Mr. Wilson is here to protect us or not, they'll kill all of us, too."

"I'm not going to let myself get caught, Violet," I countered, keeping my voice low so as not to add kindling to the fire she wanted to start. "Once I'm in the woods, I'll be as quiet as a mouse."

She rolled her eyes and began to sniffle again. I turned for Daisy.

"Doesn't that sound reasonable?" I asked.

She sighed before pulling back her thick blond hair. "I think Vi has a point. You're doing this so we'll all be safe. And I understand that." Several nods accentuated her pause. "But the opposite outcome needs to be examined as well. The one where you never come back."

She turned and faced me directly. "That isn't what you want to have happen, Bob. We all know it. You need to think this through more. Maybe give it another month or so."

Glancing back at Lettie, the disagreement I hoped to find wasn't there.

"In another month, they could attack us again," I stated. "What happens then? How are we any further ahead by not bringing the fight to them, right now?"

"You won't be dead," Violet snarled. "There's always that."

I glowered at the teen. "You're confidence in my abilities is overwhelming and fills my heart with pride."

She bolted up from her chair. "First," she shoved her finger at me, "you get your hand damn near shot off and almost bleed to death. Next," another finger poked my direction, "you get shot in the side and again, almost die. You lived two times when you had help. How do you think you're going to fare all alone in the woods, shot to hell?"

I raised my hands up, signaling for a truce. The best I got was her arms slapping around her waist.

"I'm not going to get shot," I said, trying to console Daisy more than Violet. If I could win her over, I'd have two of the three on my side. "I won't be in the open; no one will even know I'm there. I'm going to be careful. I'm going to come back."

Daisy again forced a smile. Again, she failed, instead coming across as defeated. "All Vi is saying, all I'm saying is this... we don't want you to die, Bob. Please try to understand our point of view."

"Hell, we're all going to die someday," Lettie added, picking up a new piece of clothing for mending. "You just don't need to rush into it. That's all."

Zero for three. What a terrible idea this had been. Now even *I* began to wonder if I was coming back alive.

Day 1,022

Another week passed and still no sign of anyone, much less Wilson. Standing in the front yard, staring at the road from the south, I wondered if maybe a trip back to his farm was in order.

But that, in and of itself, was problematic.

I couldn't run the risk of leaving the women alone for the half day it would take to get to Wilson's farm and back. Though they could protect themselves, the recent attack by the stranger from the road still haunted me. The risk outweighed any reward I might gain.

If Dizzy was here, if he was still alive, I could go. But then again, if he hadn't died the past winter, none of this would have been necessary. Or would it have been?

The attack back then came like a bolt of lightning from a clear winter sky. The Barster gang caught me, everyone actually, completely off guard. Their actions couldn't be planned for, that much was a given. But if they hadn't killed my best friend, we would've been stronger, even while tightly shacked up together in this small cabin.

The largest problem was that they knew we were still alive.

Even after killing two of their gang, they had to know there were survivors. There was no way, in my mind, that they had the notion that everyone had died in that fiery blaze.

I'd left them the proof they needed, stomped neatly in the snow around the cellar door.

They knew we were alive. I knew they had to die. Before they killed every last one of us.

Later in the day, I stared out the front window, wishing and hoping Wilson would appear — even if from thin air. Many times I looked away, glancing back, expecting to see the man and his cart entering the yard. But as of late afternoon, he was still mysteriously absent.

"Watched pots never boil," Lettie crowed from the kitchen. "Watched road never produces either." That part she added with a chuckle.

I turned back to give her my attention. "Where do you suppose he is? What's keeping him?"

Lettie handed Libby a slice of unleavened bread smothered in jam. Patting the child on the head, she joined the others on the couch.

"Problems on the road, most likely," Lettie replied. "Maybe even got himself killed on the way there or back. No way to know until we hear some news."

My head slumped forward into my hand. This was getting worse by the day.

"Maybe I need a new plan," I murmured from my spot by the window. "Maybe…"

Violet sprang from the couch and hovered next to me, grinning. "Maybe you just need to forget all about going after them, right?" She nodded eagerly, peeking back at Daisy. "Maybe we just go forward with life and forget all about them, right?"

I hated to burst her bubble of hope, but I'm sure my confused look softened my words.

"They still need to die, Violet. Perhaps I just need a different approach." My words made her perma-scowl return.

"Well, that's stupid," she snarled, returning to the couch.

"All I was saying," I continued, eyeing the pouting teen, "was maybe I'm over-thinking this whole thing. If I can figure out a way to know that you're all safe, I can still go after them."

Daisy smiled disingenuously. "If you're actually worried about us, Bob, then that's not a workable plan. If you don't want us here alone, left to defend ourselves if they get past you, then I don't know if you're on the right path."

True. If even one of them got away, they'd be at the cabin in no time on horseback. By the time I returned, the fight would be well over.

"I just said it was a plan," I admitted red-faced. "I hadn't worked out all the kinks yet. Not a good plan now that it's out in the open."

The baby began crying in the bedroom. Daisy rose and motioned for Violet to stay in her spot.

"Seems like Libby isn't the best sitter yet," Daisy said, opening the bedroom door. The cries became louder. "Please put her back down, sweetie. She doesn't want to be squeezed right now." The door closed and the screaming softened.

My eyes drifted and met Violet's.

"If you die," she whispered, "you're going to break her heart." She pointed at the bedroom door several times, though I understood her without further directions. "And then what will happen? To her? To Libby? To me?"

Folding her arms across her chest, she turned to stare out the back window.

"Why are you so absolutely certain I'm going to die, Violet? Huh?"

I saw her head shake slightly. "Because I've seen you do battle. And you aren't very good at it."

I glanced at Lettie; the old woman shrugged. "The girl has a point," she squawked.

Yeah, but this time was going to be different. I could feel it in my bones. Even if they all lacked confidence in my skills, I was going to win this time.

At least I hoped so.

Day 1,025

Wilson finally showed up mid-afternoon. It had been almost two weeks since his son had left with Marge, and almost a full week past when I had expected him. And from the dour look on his face, I figured he brought trouble with him.

I decided to forego the formalities of a cordial greeting.

"Where you been?" I asked in a tone that couldn't be mistaken for anything but pissed. "You should have been here a week ago."

He stopped just in front of me and lowered the wagon handle to the ground. Wiping his brow with the back of his hand, he plopped into a lawn chair adjacent to me.

"We got problems," he replied, sounding like the tired old man he was. "Some big problems."

I felt my face tighten as I looked away. Thus far, we were alone. That probably wouldn't last long.

"I don't need problems, Wilson. I need supplies, and your help here while I go after Barster. Do we have a problem there?"

His head nodded slowly. "Yep."

Great. Not only were there issues, I was going to have to

pull each one from the stubborn old man.

I decided to tackle this head on. "Okay, let's start with why you're late."

Sighing first, he gave me his story. Johnny was held up at the fish camp for an extra day while someone rounded up the required supplies. Fine, that was one day. Next, he spoke of issues on the road. Two days of heavy rain forced his son to hole up in an abandoned building, waiting for the rain to abate.

We were up to three and my patience was wearing thin.

Then, the road bandits came. Luckily, they didn't catch the boy off-guard. He saw their blockade from a mile or so away, which caused him to take alternate routes. Roads that he wasn't familiar with. He lost another day heading the wrong direction because of overcast skies.

We were getting close, almost to seven.

"Then he came upon trouble just north of Covington," Wilson informed me. "Couldn't really say if it was a war, or a siege, or whatever. All he knows is that there was a battle there. At least that's what he assumed from the gunfire he heard."

I really didn't give a damn of what was happening to the Weston's and their crew up north. What I really needed to know was if it was safe for me to proceed with my plan. But therein lied the trouble.

"Think Barster was involved in the trouble up there?" I asked. I hoped the answer would be a firm and direct no. But I feared otherwise.

Wilson shrugged, chasing a fly or two away. "No idea. Johnny said he saw a dozen people meeting in the woods just to the northwest of town. Couldn't get close enough to identify anyone though. Not safe."

I sucked in a breath and released a low moan.

"Shit," I seethed. "It'd be stupid to go after them if they're up in Covington. How long ago did Johnny see this?"

"Two, maybe three days back now," he answered, sounding like he didn't care about it himself. "Should be over, the way I see it. But that could be problematic for your…plan."

"Only if they win and take up residence in Covington," I replied, feeling a bad headache coming on. "And then they'll have larger numbers, more strength."

"Yep," Wilson drawled, nodding as he did.

"And then they could come and wipe us out at will. Probably even overrun your place."

"Yep." For a man who faced an uncertain future, he seemed awfully nonchalant about the whole thing. "And there's another problem, with the supplies from the fish camp."

Openmouthed, I shook my head. I had thought this man's return would set me free to do what I needed to do. But it seemed that wasn't in the cards.

I stared at the bald man, refusing to believe his news.

"And when did they change their policy on this?" I asked, sounding as if he had something to do with it.

"Since the last time Johnny and Jimmy were up there. Sometime late last fall." His reply suggested he took no offense from my words.

Wow, another kick in the teeth. Not exactly what we needed.

"Lettie!" I hollered. "Can you come out here?"

The door opened even before my echo died in the woods.

"I was listening in," she said, taking a spot next to me on the bench.

"How much did you hear?" I asked.

She grinned at me. "All of it."

"So you know we got screwed on the trade then."

Her head shook several times.

"According to what I heard Thaddeus say," she nodded at him, "we got half up front. The other half comes when

Marge fulfills her six-month contract. I get it."

In my defense, we all got it. People had shown up at fish camps for the past few years, the handler receiving their body weight in supplies. And as crafty people do, they'd stay a week or two and then sneak off, back to the family member or village mates who had dropped them off. Several weeks passed and the same shell game was performed at the next fish camp up the road. And on and on and on.

It took a year or two, but the camps wised up to the ploy. Unfortunately, we paid the price.

"How much did we get?" Lettie inquired, peeking at the back of the cart.

"Fifty-four pounds total," Wilson answered automatically.

That meant kind-hearted Marge weighed a little less than 110 pounds when she arrived in Ontonagon. It seemed a little low to me, but I'm sure the scales worked in the favor of their masters.

Pushing to my knees, I rose and tore the tarp away from the cart. Fifty-four pounds of staples sure didn't look like much. But it was what we got. Lettie appeared next to me.

"Is this enough to last until nearly winter?" I asked, searching her face.

"It'll have to be," she answered, poking at a bag of flour…

or sugar…or something. "It's what we got."

"And there's more to talk about," I added, leaning over the cart.

She nodded. "I heard. How about I make some flapjacks for dinner and we talk about it afterwards?"

I wasn't very hungry. Nevertheless, flapjacks did sound good. Even though yet another thing had turned to crap.

Day 1,025 - continued

"It's mid-June, best anyone can tell," Violet began, licking the last of her treat from the brown plate. She poked her head up and looked at the stove. "Is there anymore cobbler, Lettie?"

With what I figured were limited ingredients, Lettie had whipped up an awfully good treat. The berries she used were hard and small, but the concoction did not lack taste.

"Mid-June," I repeated, picking up on Violet's lead. "And the time to strike is now, not next year at this time."

Daisy sighed loudly before looking up. "But they might be up in Covington," she said, licking her fork. "If you go now, you may come back empty-handed. That *is* a possibility, right?"

Against every belief I held dear to me, I nodded, but only slightly.

"And Mr. Wilson has people who can tell him what's going on," Daisy continued. "And he'll let you know when the time may be right."

Yes, yes, and again, yes. But time was wasting…at least in my mind.

She smiled and rubbed my hand lovingly. "Then you wait.

Until at least you know what you're up against. It's safer that way. And you'll know if their numbers have increased." She smiled at our tablemates. "I think this is all for the best, don't you all?"

Lettie nodded. Violet gave me the stink eye.

"Damn straight," the girl answered. "This way we know where you are and know that you're safe."

Oh sure, they all had this figured out. Or so they thought. Time to get some fresh air out of the room.

"And what if they amass a larger army and attack while we're sitting around with our thumbs up our asses?" I asked, using the bitterest tone I could muster with this group. We did all have to live together…for a while at least.

That got them to shut up. And it wiped those smug looks off their face.

"Tomorrow you start on Plan B," Lettie stated, pushing way from the table to serve us all seconds.

I had a hard time not laughing at her. "And what, may I ask, is Plan B?"

Winking at me first, she hoisted a double piece of cobbler onto my plate. "Starting tomorrow you'll figure that out, won't you?"

They all shared a good chuckle. Why would they care about

Plan B? They were just happy Plan A was grounded for now.

Day 1,030

I wasted five days wallowing in my own pity. Four actually. Fixing holes in the roof took up the middle day. My female cabin friends pointed out their approximate locations. And oh were they happy.

I wanted revenge in the worst way. But I really didn't see it as revenge. To me, it was a proactive attack to defend my family and myself. To defend our home.

I began each day with a stare down. My opponent? The road. Specifically, the road from the south. And each morning, the empty road claimed its victory.

Wilson told us it would be at least a week before he came back. Since I believed good news traveled fast, I expected him at any moment…every day.

I also spent my time chopping and stacking wood. The previous winter we had been low by the end of the heating season. I figured we needed another cord above and beyond what I'd cut previously.

Which kept me busy, and in front of the cabin.

Which turned out to be a lucky break for us all.

***

Mid-day, I noticed movement in the brush across the road, pausing from my wood stacking to study it closer. Seeing nothing more, I dismissed it as a deer or maybe even Chester or one of his family members. The wolves had been active lately, still hungry after a long cold winter.

An hour passed, maybe two. I worked up a good sweat making dozens of trips from the front of the cabin to the rear. At some point, Daisy sat a cup of water out for me and disappeared back inside.

I paused, taking in the beautiful, sunny early summer weather. If nothing, No Where was a beautiful place to call home. *Home,* I mused, *what a strange concept.*

For almost the first year and a half in Michigan's remote northern reaches, getting back to my original home was all I ever thought of. Oh sure, there were breaks in that thought pattern. I had to take time out to survive, sleep, hunt and get shot several times. Other than that, Joliet, Illinois and my wife Shelly were forefront on my mind.

Perhaps Marge's family swayed me from that thinking. Or the arrival of and love given by Daisy and Libby. Maybe it was even something as simple as Dizzy's friendship that eventually made those dreams fade away like a bad cut. Whatever it was, No Where was where I belonged. Where I would live out my remaining days. Where I would eventually die and be buried, or fed to my wolf pack as dinner.

Had I given up on all other life? Was this all that was left in the world for me? Was there anything left beyond the borders of my roaming that was better? A place that had more food, more supplies, more decent folks?

Lost in my thoughts, the voice from the north side of my open yard froze me dead in my tracks and made me drop my water.

"Hello there," the voice called out.

I spun and drew my 45 on a younger man with long hair and a longer beard. His dark eyes focused tightly on me. Both hands raised, as if that fooled me. In his right hand he carried a stick with a white rag tied to the end.

"I just want to talk," he continued calmly. "I don't want trouble."

That's what they all said.

Day 1,030 - continued

Since he didn't appear to have a weapon on him, I let my gun hang by my side. That didn't mean he didn't have two or three friends hiding somewhere close. No, that most likely was the case. I chose to focus my attention on the immediate threat standing in front of me.

"Didn't mean to scare you, man," he said, smiling seemingly sincerely. "I know you're working hard, so I won't keep you long."

Remaining silent, I cast a glance over the road again to the spot where I'd seen movement earlier. Again, nothing. I quickly peeked behind me. Nothing. I turned back to my visitor. He wasn't alone, and he certainly wasn't fooling me.

"Can we talk?" he asked, not smiling as much anymore. "Like reasonable people?"

I doubted his sincerity. Like everyone else from the road, he wanted something. Regardless of what that something was, it was mine and he wasn't getting it.

Taking two steps toward the man, I raised my weapon. Leveling it on his chest, his smile faded slightly.

"I'm not in a very talkative mood," I replied, circling him

for a weapon check. "Pull your shirt up so I can see what you have tucked in your waistband."

With his left hand, he obliged my request. He appeared unarmed, but that didn't mean anything.

"I'm not carrying, man," he said. "I don't need to."

I felt his back and chest in one last search. "Everyone needs to these days, pal. Everyone."

Back in front of him, I noticed his smile again. No, it was more of a grin. Like he knew something I didn't. Yeah, I bet he did.

"So, what do you want to talk about?" I demanded, lowering my gun again. "Make it fast; I've got a lot to accomplish today."

He nodded, still grinning. "A man with a plan, I like that. I think I like you. It's Bob, right?"

Damn it. Either he was from Covington, or someone up the road had told him my name.

"You see," he continued, his hands now hanging by his sides, "we've been watching you for a couple days. Watching and waiting."

His hand rose to his chin as he stared off into the blue sky. "Let's see. We've got Bob, and Daisy, and Lettie, and Violet, and Libby." He snapped his fingers. "I'm sorry; I don't think I know the baby's name...yet."

He knew way too much for my comfort. While I didn't doubt he and his friends, hiding somewhere nearby, hadn't heard our sometimes loud conversations, there was no reason to rule out that he was part of the trouble in Covington. Maybe Susan Weston had sent him, a kind of pre-attack attack.

"You're not going to be around long enough to find out her name," I replied, fingering my gun as I watched behind him for any movement. "And what's your name, if I dare ask?"

Opening his arms, he bowed slightly. "I am your humble servant. You can call me Carmen."

I inched closer. "You want to live to see tomorrow, Carmen?"

His eyebrows flashed for a split second, and then his grin broadened. "Kill me and my crew kills all of you. Don't worry; they'll keep you alive long enough to watch the rest of your cute little group die first. Among other things."

Yeah, he meant trouble. And in a big way.

"So what do you want from us, Carmen?"

He tapped my chest once. "Here's what I need, Bob. I need you, the old woman, and the little blonde girl to pack up and get out of here. Get out and never come back, Bob. We'll take care of everything else for you. Don't you worry about that."

His words shot a bolt of adrenaline through my chest and out to my extremities. I wasn't about to show him any fear. No, that's what he wanted.

I let out a small amused huff. "I don't think so, Carmen. I've battled plenty to keep my place. You're just a number to me. And to be honest…" I paused to let my words sink in, "I've lost count long ago of those who've lost."

He nodded like he understood, but I didn't think he'd been swayed. "There's no reason to start a war here, man. I don't want to kill you, Bob. I sure as hell don't want to kill that old woman or that little girl. Nevertheless, I want your place, your women and your supplies.

"You see, I've been living off the land long enough, I figure." He looked away towards the road, then slowly back at me. "I deserve a break. My crew deserves one, too. There were eight of us not long ago. Now we're down to three. We learned a lot in our last battle. We didn't win, but we gained valuable knowledge. And we're not leaving, just so you know."

These had to be the clowns who tried to take Covington. Though I wasn't sure which direction this one had come, he was on the north side of my property. If he came from the north, that meant he'd battled the Weston's…and lost.

I moved so close our noses nearly touched. "If you and what's left of your gang want to see tomorrow, I'd suggest you move on. Because that's your only choice if you want to live. You don't know what we have for firepower inside. You got no clue what you're up against. So why don't you move along."

He stared at me, his lip sliding back and forth. I knew he wasn't part of Barster's bunch. There were no horses. None that I could see at least. I also didn't think Clyde Barster was the kind of fellow that would let a sleazy man like this do his talking.

He poked my chest. "You've been warned," he said, none too pleased. He actually sounded angry. It made me wonder if he really wanted a fight. He was probably just trying to scare me off.

"Get ready for a battle," he whispered just before turning around.

I *was* ready, fool.

Day 1,030 - continued

The first shot rang out from the brush across the road. Carmen was still walking away, still on my property. But the hail of gunfire didn't allow me to draw and get a bead on him.

I dove inside just as an explosion came out of the south woods. It had to have been a shotgun because I heard multiple shots hit the screen door as I jerked it shut behind me. Two holes in the aluminum confirmed my belief. Someone had a shotgun with buckshot.

Looking around from the floor, I noticed Lettie kneeling close to me with her 30-30 in hand.

"Saw that bastard come off the road," she said in a hushed tone, peeking out the front window. "Heard everything he said. I had Violet take Libby and Hope into the bedroom and get on the far side of the bed. I told her to pull the mattress over them. They should be safe."

I got to my feet, kneeling by the wall between the front window and the screen door. The bedroom door was shut. Good. One way or another, three of us were going to be safe. But we were missing someone.

I was about to ask Lettie when I heard movement to my

left. Glancing over, I saw Daisy. Crouching by the cupboards, she was busy loading shells into Dizzy's 20-gauge.

"You okay?" I asked Daisy. Her only response was a nervous look and a quick nod. She was all right, and ready for the fight.

Lettie inched closer to me. "Think there's really three of them?" she asked.

"Maybe, maybe not." I peeked out through the damaged screen, trying to pick up movement. Nothing. That was good enough for now.

Studying the rest of the room, I discovered places we were vulnerable. The rear window wasn't large, but still, someone could easily pop up and fire inside through that access.

"Daisy," I whispered, "crawl over and draw the blinds on the back window." It wasn't perfect, but it prevented an unfettered look through the window.

The front window was mostly glass; two small side windows had screens and both were open. We could use those for firing positions. I wanted the front door open for a while yet. It gave us more firing access and I could peek over the frame and see what was going on outside.

The only window that truly worried me was the one in the bedroom. I had no way of knowing whether it was open or closed. Since it faced the road, I figured I'd be able to see anyone approaching it.

We were set up as best as we could be. And that would have to do.

Two men dashed along the north tree line, just inside the brush. They were trying to flank us and get at our rear. I pushed the door open and clicked the safety off on the 45. Pulling the trigger, the gun jerked six or seven times in my hand. Their movements halted, followed by moaning from the brush. At least one was down.

Looking back, I saw the scared looks on both Lettie's and Daisy's faces. That and Daisy covering her ears. The echo of the gunfire from the home had been loud, so I couldn't blame her.

Crying started in the bedroom. Probably from the shots. I motioned to Daisy with my head.

"Check on them," I instructed. "Be sure they're all right." She crept and pushed the door open, disappearing from my view.

I focused back where I'd seen the men. Something was going on in the brush. One of them, if not both, had to be writhing on the ground.

"I just need a peek at them to know what happened," I whispered back to Lettie. "You cover me. I'm just going to push this screen door open a little so I can get a better view."

Lettie took position on the far side of the front window, her gun pointed outward.

I opened it a crack at first. I figured any movement of the door would bring a hail of gunfire, but none came. So I opened it a little more.

Because I was so low to the ground, I couldn't see much. With no shots to warn me otherwise, I inched a little higher, then a little more.

Standing bent at the waist, I could see two sets of feet kicking about in the brush. That meant two down, one to go. And he had to be the fellow with the scattergun behind me.

I knelt again and checked to the south. Using the door as cover, I peered into the lush green brush, searching for something out of place. If he had a shotgun, he couldn't be too deep in. But as best as I could tell, there was no one out there.

Seeing his two comrades fall may have motivated the third assailant to hightail it for the next county. I kept looking, searching, probing each hole in the dense canopy for any sign of life. *Maybe the war was already over*, I thought. *Would've been nice if the remaining fellow at least said goodbye.*

I turned again to get a better look at the wounded. Checking my rear one last time, I dared a step away from the cover of the door. Still nothing. This was over. We had won.

Three steps towards the injured men, I heard a twig snap behind me.

Shit, it wasn't over.

Day 1,030 - continued

The shotgun blast shattered the otherwise calm woodlands. I felt two burning spots in my back as I tumbled to the ground, spinning to point my weapon at the shooter. He wasn't there; I couldn't find him anywhere.

"Why don't you drop your gun, Bob," a voice called out from behind. It was not just any voice, it was Carmen's voice.

"And why don't you have anyone else with a gun toss them outside," he continued, sounding joyful for the situation. But why shouldn't he have felt that way? He was winning.

Someone laid the 30-30 beside me. Looking back, I saw Lettie. Lettie and a half-blasted away screen door. That explained why the blast hadn't ripped me in two.

"Any more?" Carmen called out.

Lettie gave me a defeated look. "No, that's all. Just the two we have." *Good girl*, I thought.

"John's gonna come from the south, and I'm going to approach from the north," Carmen stated. I could hear him moving through the brush. "If either of you does anything stupid, you both die."

My back burned worse than I thought it could. I'd fallen in

the dirt and could feel grit grinding against the wounds like sandpaper. I heard men approach from both sides.

"Guess I didn't get you both in the brush over there," I said, wincing. "Too bad."

"Oh you got both of them," Carmen replied, sounding disappointed. "There were four of us though. I was kind of counting on you buying into that."

Sure, play to the stupid man. The guy in the dirt without a gun.

"And I think you made mortal shots on both of them," he continued. "They're not even kicking anymore."

"Too bad I don't get a bead on you," I shouted. "John and I could have made a deal."

Carmen cut off the sun with his shadow. "I got a deal for you, Bob. I'm going to kill you right in front of your friends. Then they'll know who they're *dealing* with."

His friend pointed the long shotgun at my head. "Now okay, boss?"

I saw both of them laugh. That wasn't good. None of it was.

"Let's haul everyone outside so they can see the end of Bob Reiniger, John." Carmen answered with a grin. "Wouldn't want anyone to miss this."

"I got a question for you before you kill me. Who sent you here?" I wasn't trying to stall. I just needed to know before I died.

Carmen knelt next to me and pulled my hair, forcing my face to look at him. "Friend of yours— Susan Weston. She said you'd be excited to have company. Claimed you'd want to share your food and such." He peeked at his shotgun-toting ghoul and chuckled. "Once you were dead, that is."

Both men laughed. I got it. I lose, they win. Shit.

Carmen did a quick lap inside the cabin and brought all the occupants outside to line up. I suppose it was to watch my execution, not that I'd see much of it once his henchman pulled the trigger.

Across from me the group stood, all but Lettie crying. Hope was in full scream mode, mostly because Violet was shaking from her sobs. Daisy held Libby in front of her, face inward towards her shirt. Her eyes squeezed shut, then open again, both wanting to be there for me and not wanting to watch the end.

Carmen paced before them. "Now, I don't have anything against you all. And I sure don't have anything against Bob here." He smiled at me as if we were pals or something.

"But Bob's going to be a problem if we let him live," he continued, stroking his facial hair. "And since I'm down to one hired man, I can't afford to let problems live."

Daisy pushed Libby to Lettie and inched forward. "Please don't do this," she begged, pulling on Carmen's arm, "I'm sure we can work something out."

The evil one stared and nodded at her. "Something tells me you're Daisy, right?" She refused to acknowledge him. "Susan said I should kill you, too. But…" his eyes roamed her thin body as his lips formed into a sneer, "I think I want you alive. You could be a fun one. You and that other taller gal." His head flipped towards Violet.

"Please don't," Daisy continued to beg. "Please let Bob live. I'll do anything if you'll just let him go."

Carmen took a step and peered down into her weepy face. "You'll do anything if I kill him, too. Wouldn't want anything to happen to that little girl of yours, now would we?"

"Let's get this over with, Carmen," his man stated in a bored tone. "I'm hungry. And I need a nap and someone to snuggle with." They shared a demonic chuckle.

He spun and knelt next to me. "Okay, it's time to say goodbye, Bob. Playtime's over."

John's gun rose and my family let out a collective scream. I noticed the man's brown teeth, his scarred face, the left eye that looked slightly out of alignment with the right. I refused to look at my group, instead facing my executioner.

"Get it over with, asshole," I spewed, watching his grin grow.

"Gladly." And the safety snapped free.

This was really happening, I thought — perhaps my last.

Day 1,030 - continued

The first shot rang out and I flinched, shutting my eyes. I felt a spray of something across my face. Wherever he'd hit me didn't hurt, which seemed extremely odd to me. A second shot followed the first and more spray. Still no pain. Was this guy hitting me somewhere without nerves? Was this death or torture?

When something hard fell on me, my eyes shot opened. Staring at the face, what was left of it at least, I saw Carmen's blank eyes staring back. The blood pouring from his head caused me to roll over and push away, jumping up from the ground.

Blood covered my shirt. His blood or mine, I wasn't sure.

I glanced right, another dead body. Sticking out beneath it was a shotgun. That had to be John. Back to my left was Carmen. Both were dead, both shot in the head.

My group, every one of them still lay sprinkled about on the ground. Lettie was covering Violet and Hope; Daisy was on top of Libby. Strangely, I was the only one on my feet.

I noticed someone approached from the road. Whoever it was had a rifle leveled at me. My hands went up instinctively.

However, once I spotted his bald head and long strides, I lowered them back down. Our savior strolled towards us stone-faced: Thaddeus Wilson.

"Johnny told me there was trouble on the road," he called out, kicking both men to be sure they were dead. "Guess he was right."

I felt like hugging the man. "Holy shit," I whopped. "Am I glad you showed up when you did. These idiots were really going to kill me."

As Wilson helped Lettie and Violet up, I did the same for Daisy and Libby. Instantly Daisy threw her arms around my shoulders and hugged me.

"My God, my God, my God," Daisy kept repeating. "Oh my God. I am so thankful you're alive." She let go of me and hugged Wilson's mid-section just as tight. "And thank you Mr. Wilson, for saving us."

Lettie and Daisy smiled and clambered on with Wilson about the events as Violet circled around my back. I felt one of her thin fingers digging in behind me. *Probably nothing good would come of that*, I thought.

"I count five spots," she cried, a little more hysterical than the situation deserved. "Six — there's one on your lower back."

I turned and faced her since she was already weeping. "It's nothing, Violet. Barely scratches; they don't even hurt."

"But that's a lot of blood," Daisy said from behind. "We need to get you inside."

"Really, I'm okay." I was just so damn happy not to be dead that I didn't care about a few holes in my back.

"Buckshot?" Wilson asked. I nodded. "But not at close range?" I grinned and winked. "Still needs to be cleaned up. Better get at it."

Getting another hug from Daisy, I agreed. Lettie led us all inside, including Wilson. He stopped me just before we got in.

"That was a fairly close call, Bob," he said in a low tone. "I don't know how that would've turned out if I hadn't shown up."

I agreed as he gave me a hardy pat on the back and I let out a whine. Okay, these pellets hurt a little. But I was still alive, and that's all that mattered.

Inside, Wilson explained how he had come to save us. Though I expected a great tale of running and chasing ending with him steadying against a tree for good shot, it was nothing that exciting.

He had posted Johnny up the road a mile north of Lettie's

property since the day after his return from Covington. His reason was simple; he didn't want anything happening to his granddaughter or her mother. Violet's protection saved me.

He claimed he was a half mile from us when the first shots rang out. Instead of sprinting to our rescue, like I thought he might, he only picked up his pace a little.

"No sense in running if I was going to find you all dead," he reasoned.

He only arrived when Carmen's gunman drew his final bead on my lying body. Settling his sights on John's head, he squeezed the trigger. Once sure he was dead, Wilson disposed of Carmen.

Problem solved, Thaddeus Wilson style. Thank God.

He left to fetch some medicine for me. Even before he hit the blacktop, Lettie pulled the last of the seven pieces of buckshot from my back.

"Now let's clean these wounds," she said, the last piece of metal clunking into the white dishpan. "I don't think any of these are life-threatening." She slapped my back, a little too hard it felt. Or maybe I was being a baby.

"I'm fine," I said, eyeing Violet, who was eyeing me. "Give me a few days to heal and I'll be ready to get back at what I need to do."

"Yeah, right," Violet spewed. "Once again, your blood is flowing. How about you take a break from all this crap and just sit around for a while."

Daisy circled behind me, rubbing my shoulder. "Maybe that's a good idea, Bob. Let yourself heal up before you think about doing anything else."

She kissed my cheek and I smiled at her. "Sure, I can do that. It's probably a good idea."

My two conspirators exchanged a knowing, almost devious look. But that was okay. I lied to them. I wasn't sitting around for a second longer than necessary, no matter what they might have thought.

Day 1,038

I finished throwing up in a bucket and flopped onto my back on the couch. Bad idea. The pain shot me back up into a sitting position.

"And here I was worried about Clyde Barster killing you," Lettie laughed above me. "Hell, the infection will get you long before Barster gets his hands on you."

I rubbed my forehead, feeling the heat pour from my body. This was crap, 130 percent crap. I thought I was in the clear after Lettie removed the shot from my back. A few days on the couch and I'd be fine.

Little did I know that even with the penicillin Wilson brought as a precaution that an infection would follow. That was not some little run-of-the-mill, come-and-go infection. No, it was a grand-mal infection.

Daisy trotted up with a glass of water and more pills. "Here, sweetie. It's time again. Maybe that nasty infection is finally getting out of you."

I pointed at the bucket. "Only thing coming out right now is lunch," I moaned. "When is this going to pass?"

"When it passes," Lettie crowed, "or when you finally die

from it." Her suppressed laugh didn't help.

"You're better today," Daisy continued, rubbing a bare shoulder. "And I'll bet you'll feel even better tomorrow."

This sucked big time. Not only was I devoid of any energy that would've allowed me to get up from the couch, I couldn't even stomach the idea of going outside. If attackers ambushed us right now, the best I could hope for was to be killed first.

Violet came out of the bedroom and shut the door quietly. Seeing me in my suffering state, she smiled. That little bitch.

"And how's our patient today?" Her voice, dripping with honey, her smile fake and wide. As she stepped through the doorway, she paused. Her smile faded and she covered her nose as she got close enough to get a whiff of the bucket. Grabbing its metal handle, she made toward the door. "I'm sorry," she called back through a smile. "Maybe next week you'll be well enough to get up and move around. Maybe."

I'd be getting on my feet again, and soon, if I had anything to say about it. Then another wave of nausea ran through me and I puked on the bare floor.

Libby let out a loud "EWWWW!" and Daisy hustled over with an old red plaid dishtowel and another cup of tepid water.

Maybe another day, two at the most, I thought, sinking onto my side.

Day 1,055

Sitting in the warm summer sunshine, I let Libby chase flies away from my scabbed bare back. They could bite me for all I cared. Daisy didn't appreciate the loud bursts of profanity that followed each shovel-nosed extraction by the black and deer flies though. We compromised: I'd let Libby swat me as much as she wanted and I wouldn't swear…much.

I'd lost track of time since my latest losing gun battle. The others reminded me how happy they were I was alive. While that helped a little, I hated being an invalid. Honestly, I was the worst patient in the history of No Where.

For 10 days I laid on the couch, sometimes of the world and sometimes not. For the first seven, I couldn't keep anything down, not flatbread, not water, not even spit. Everything came up within 10 minutes of ingestion. While that was lots of fun, my focus was on the fever that gave me the strangest dreams of my life.

The world came to me one morning, alive and full of sun and warmth. Someone had put me in my bed, the twin in the back room. Why the baby wasn't there I wasn't sure. But everything was quiet, clean, and warm, and the world felt good.

My scars had healed. Probably all of the coconut oil Lettie had rubbed on my body. My left side looked as new and fresh as my right. Gone was the ugly wound and raised flesh born when the shotgun slug tried to tear me in two.

I checked my back in a mirror. Those marks, too, had disappeared. Not one of the seven remained. *Amazing*, I thought. A little rest and some much-needed sleep had really done the trick. I needed to thank everyone for their help.

Opening the bedroom door, I flexed my left hand. Slowly I raised it before my face and discovered something wonderful. Against all odds, and everything I knew to be possible in nature, my left pinky had grown back. I marveled at its perfection, how it moved in harmony with the others as if it had never gone missing from the gunshot wound.

This was going to be a great day.

Golden waves of sunshine filled the main room of the cabin. The air temperature was perfect and allowed me to roam around bare-chested. My feet felt anew on the wood floor, sensing every crook and crack. And they didn't hurt, not one bit.

I was refreshed and ready for whatever needed to be done. And I knew what came next. I was certain now was the time to go after our attackers and right the wrongs they'd brought upon us.

But that's what made me stop. Where were the rest of *us*?

I listened for voices; perhaps they were just outside, working in the garden. *That would make sense on such a wondrous day*, I thought. Peeking out the window, I saw no one. And that bothered me.

If they had taken a walk together, the group ran the risk of running into road scum. That would make them vulnerable and that was not a good plan.

"What are you looking at?" a voice behind me asked. I turned to find Violet and a young lady standing behind me, hand in hand. At first, I thought it was Libby. However, the young lady had dark hair and looked to be six or seven years old.

"Where is everyone else?" I asked, confused by the girl and the dress that Violet wore. The long green and blue plaid sleeveless dress hugged her now mature form. She wasn't 15 any longer. She looked more like that of a 20-something woman.

"Everyone else is gone, Bob," she answered, releasing the girl's hand and walking towards me. "It's just you, me and

Hope now. It has been for a while. Probably will be forever."

She hugged me tightly. "I've missed you while you were gone. I was worried you might never come back."

I didn't understand, not a word of it. "Where'd I go?"

She looked up at me, stroking my clean-shaven face, running her fingers through my short hair.

"Oh, here and there," she replied, standing on her tiptoes, gently kissing my lips. "But everything's okay now. Everything is as it should be."

She kissed me again, more passionate this time. As if…

"What are you doing?" I asked. Why I didn't try to pull away, I didn't know. But I didn't.

She kissed me again, this time with an opened mouth. This caused me to think about pushing her away, but still I didn't. I had no idea why I allowed it to continue.

When the passion ended, she led me to the table. But not a table I was familiar with. This was a large, beautifully set table with dishes of orange and gold and a stark-white tablecloth. A tall glass of cold beer waited at my spot.

I sipped the IPA, enjoying the mild taste, allowing it to swirl in my mouth before I swallowed. I almost cried as the familiar taste tickled my throat. It was perfect.

Hope sat a plate in front of me. On it was a large steak

smothered in mushrooms, just as I liked. Next to the steak was a pile of baby potatoes, covered in melting bright yellow butter. At the top of the plate sat a pile of bright green Brussels sprouts with hunks of bacon.

Everything I loved, cooked perfectly and served with a smile.

I stared at my hostesses as they stood over me. "Where's yours?" I asked, cutting my first bite of bloody steak. Somehow, Violet knew just how I liked it.

She sat on one side of me as Hope took a place opposite of her. "We don't eat anymore, Bob. We don't have to."

I stuffed the meat in my mouth and chewed. Waiting for the flavor to caress my palate, I smiled at her. "Why don't you eat? You mean you ate earlier?"

"No," she replied, stroking my hand, kissing my moving lips again.

Only then did I realize that the steak had no taste. Leaning forward, I inhaled the steam from the meat, potatoes and vegetables. Nothing registered.

I looked back at Hope, but now she appeared tired and worn. Dark circles appeared where none were only moments ago. A glance at Violet showed the same. I spit the meat back onto the plate.

Shaking my head, I spun to face Violet. "What's going on here? Where is everyone? Why doesn't anything have taste or smell?"

I pulled at her hands while she smiled back at me. I noticed her teeth were gray and split. Several were missing.

"We're all dead, Bob," she answered in a placid tone. "You weren't here to protect us. We all died. Lettie and Libby first. Then Daisy. Hope and I held out as long as we could, but those mean men killed us in the end."

"What about me?!" I yelled, now able to get a decent breath into my lungs.

Hope stroked my shoulder. "You never recovered from your wounds, Daddy. You died, too. Come outside and I'll show you where we buried everyone."

In an instant, we were standing by the road, the three of us holding hands. But their hands were boney now and even my skin had begun to gray.

In front of us were dozens of tombstones. I counted six rows of eight, far too many for just the few of us.

"That one is Libby's," Hope said, noting the far one towards the end. "And there's Daisy's, and Dizzy's, and Frank's."

She led me by the hand as the rows and markers grew in

numbers.

"Your mom and dad are buried over here," she continued. She may have been dying in front of me, but Hope's voice was as sweet as the winds through the pines. "Bud, his wife and children are back there. And here's yours."

The ground was all dead and full of bugs burrowing up to the surface. According to what I could tell, I'd been dead for a while.

"Where's Violet's, and yours, Hope?" I asked somberly.

Violet took my hand and led me across the road, deep into the woods.

"We died here," she said, pointing at an area covered with shrubs and moss. "We have no graves, no markers. This is where they left us."

What life was inside of my soul moments before had left me. "I'm sorry," I murmured. "I'm so sorry."

Violet kissed my bare arm. "It's okay, darling. Chester and his family had a feast with what was left of us. It's the way it needed to be."

Staring at the spot, I realized suddenly that I was alone. Violet and Hope had left me. I moved brush and noticed a few dulled white bones to my left. Behind them, a wolf, perhaps Chester, chewed on a ball.

My death led to the downfall of my family. Not just my blood family, or Shelly, but everyone. I was a fool for risking their lives for my selfish motives. But there was no way to change it.

Day 1,055 - continued

"Sweetheart, are you all right?"

Daisy's voice caused me to jump, returning me to the present, away from my nightmare. I stared at her, memorizing each pore of her skin, every lash above her eyes, the small gaps between her tiny teeth.

"Yeah," I answered, shaking away my fright. "Just thinking of a weird dream I had a few nights back, that's all."

"I brought you some water," she continued, sitting next to me and opposite Libby. She smiled graciously and gazed at the beautiful day surrounding us. "The flies aren't too bad for you, are they?"

I smiled at her as well. "No, not bad at all. And my little helper here is doing a good job keeping away the few that show up."

She circled an arm through mine. "I'm so glad you're feeling better. I was worried about you." She kissed my arm gently. "A few more weeks and you should be as good as new."

Yeah, two more weeks of sitting around, watching others do the jobs I should be doing. Not my way.

"Any word from Wilson as to the Barster gang?" I asked.

I felt her head dig in deeper to my arm; her squeeze tightening. "No," she replied softly, almost sounding upset. "He's had his boys check and no one has seen hide nor hair of them."

Together we watched Lettie and Violet in the garden. On their hands and knees, each plucking whatever few weeds they could find. I was amazed that even with this crappy soil, Lettie was a master at her trade.

"I suppose that's good," I continued with the subject that caused Daisy's distress. "Maybe they all bought the farm up in Covington. Or maybe they moved on."

I felt her nod against my arm, her hold on it still as tight. "Yes," she whispered, "maybe they've moved on."

We ate a late dinner by candlelight. The warm glow lit the room to an almost viewable state. The cool night air crept in slowly, forcing the day's warmth away.

"Garden's looking good," I said to my silent tablemates. "Should have the first harvest of vegetables soon from what I saw today."

A few nods as a reply, but nothing more. No one dared to peek at me, their eyes focused on their plates.

"Hopefully I can start splitting wood again within a day or

two," I added, trying to sound twice as jovial as the group deserved. "Maybe I'll just start by stacking the stuff I cut before the shoot-out. That's probably best. Don't want to push it too hard at first."

A few more nods.

Lettie finally looked up at me. "Violet and Daisy stacked that crap a few days back," she said, picking at something in her teeth. "You just rest until you're fully healed."

My turn to nod and smile. I was sick of resting and they all knew it.

"I'm gonna say something," Violet stated in a firm tone, "and I don't want anyone to bite my head off when I do." The last few eyes came up from their picked at food.

"Vi, I know what you're going to say—" Daisy tried to begin. But the teen cut her off.

"I heard you talking today," Violet began her rant. "I heard what you said. And I'm going to give you my opinion."

Crossing my arms, I pushed back from my spot. *This should be good*, I thought.

She rose from her place and began by pointing a finger my way. "You are not going after that gang. Not now, not in a few weeks, not ever. And that needs to be the end of the discussion."

I rolled my eyes and caught her vicious stare. "Oh," she continued, "I don't get a say in this? Wanna bet? I have a daughter now. She deserves to be protected."

Daisy jumped up and was quickly at her side, pulling on her arm. "Now Vi, we don't need to discuss this. At least not for a while. Please don't upset yourself. It's not worth it."

The girl spun on her friend. "Tell him how you feel, Daisy. Tell him what you told me last week."

That piqued my interest. "Yeah Daisy, tell me how you feel," I said.

She turned and faced me, fighting back tears with a watery smile. "I just think," she paused, taking a deep breath, "maybe if we talked about it. Perhaps, Bob…" The words came in sputters, forced.

"She thinks you're an idiot if you go after that gang," Violet spewed. "She doesn't want to see you die either."

I nodded slightly at Daisy. "Is that what you think?"

She came towards me, crouching beside my chair. "I never said you were an idiot. What I told Violet," she peeked back at the scowling girl, "is that, in my mind, it was a foolish thing for you to try. That's all. Just how I feel about it."

"And Lettie?" Violet added, seething a little less now.

The old woman shrugged. "You damn near get killed every

year in your own front yard. Can't see why you need to run off to do it again, somewhere else this time. That's all."

I fumed silently for a few moments. "So you're all against me going and taking care of this, instead of fighting this battle at our own home?"

Violet nodded in an exaggerated fashion. Daisy smiled, Lettie shrugged again.

"I can't promise anything," I said, keeping my voice low. I wanted to scream at them all. I wanted to bang some sense into their thick skulls. However, I also didn't want to wake the baby or frighten Libby. "But at least I know how you all feel. I appreciate your honesty."

"We just want you safe," Daisy said, kissing my cheek.

"We just want you here," Violet added, taking her place again.

And I just wanted this over with, one way or another. But that would be a delicate sell. And that would require another week of rehab and several more discussions with the most stubborn people in No Where.

Day 1,056

Our food supply was meager. Without my hunting prowess and not much from the garden yet, we were low on rations again. Unfortunately, the only thing Wilson was in good supply of was protein. And while that kept us alive, we needed something besides meat in our diet.

Lettie had little Libby pick as many dandelions as she could each and every day. The smiling girl would pick a bucket, then a second (and sometimes a third) and Lettie would thank her with a kiss and grand praise. What the old woman did with the greens gagged me, but we needed it.

In a pot of bubbling water, Lettie placed the green leaves and boiled them into a stew. It was really more of a sticky thick broth, but calling it stew made it edible. Every evening, we all had to gag a bowl of steaming hot dandelion green down our unwilling throats. And none were pleased.

"Oh my, these are even bitterer than the last batch," Daisy grimaced between bites of pork, bread and tiny spoonful of the stew. "There has to be a way to take away some of the bitterness."

Lettie pondered this, her face scrunched. "There are several ingredients to add. If I had my cupboard back at my old place, I could come up with something." She scooped a large spoonful of green slime into her mouth, swallowing it with great effort. "But that's all gone, so you'll have to make the best of it."

Violet pushed her bowl away. "I'd rather die than eat another bite of this shit." Lettie seemed unoffended by the teen's terse words.

"Now Vi," Daisy started, "we can't have little Hope growing up without a mother. So you'll have to force it down somehow."

Libby played with a piece of bread at her spot. "I can't eat mine. They make me want to throw up."

I couldn't blame the child. I had to fight the bile back with each spoonful. There had to be more, something perhaps even palatable, that nature had to offer.

"Tomorrow we'll go searching for fiddle-head ferns and wild mushrooms," Lettie offered, wiping her mouth and grinning at the green residue on her cloth napkin. "And we need Thaddeus to show up with some soap pretty soon as well. We all stink and our clothes ain't much better."

So true, I thought. *So very true.*

I had bathed shortly after my return to the world as we

knew it. The others had forgone any sort of luxury so that I could do so. Considering their other option — bathing me while passed out — Violet had thrown the biggest hissy fit she could. Something about been there, done that, paid the dues, she claimed.

We were alive, but just barely. At best, we were surviving, but again, just barely. We needed something more, and I knew that was something we all prayed for every night.

Day 1,058

Leaning on a shovel, not doing any actual work, I watched Wilson saunter up the road from the south. In his hand was a small bag, maybe the size of an old grocery bag. He wore a worried frown.

"Glad to see you upright again," he called out in his usual easy way. "Last time I checked in on you, I thought we'd need to dig a hole."

I laughed slightly, staring at the bag. "What'd you bring us?"

He nodded once at the sack. "Boys shot a couple geese late yesterday. Nate actually got one this time. We kept his. Rite of passage to eat your first kill. But this is what Jimmy and Johnny shot."

Watching as he placed the bag on the ground, I wondered what else might be on his mind. He wasn't the chatty kind, but he usually had more to say than the basic details.

I decided to ease into the topic though. "Haven't asked lately; how's Nate doing?"

Wiping his face, he looked away. "That boy is fine, growing up a lot. Missed his Ma at first, but now I can hardly keep him at the table. If he isn't hunting or trapping, he's doing chores in the barn, or tending the garden."

I'd have to remember to mention that to Violet. Though she never did ask at all about her little brother, or her mother, for that matter.

"What's got you with the worried look, if I can ask?" So much for waiting.

He first glanced at the house, then both directions on the road. Before he began, he crept in close. This had to be good, I figured.

"Got a problem," he said quietly. "Kinda a big one. Had some neighbors to the east, maybe eight miles or so. Couple days ago I went to trade them some milk for cheese. Didn't like what I found."

I felt my chest tighten. "What was that?"

Again, he peeked at the house. "Place had been robbed, picked clean," he answered in a deep tone. His eyes met mine. "And I found every last family member dead inside, all six of them. Shot in the chest."

I sucked in sharply and let it out slowly between pursed lips. "That's not good."

His head shook. "Nope. I went and warned several other families in that same area. None of them had seen any trouble in the least bit. But one fellow told me something peculiar he'd found."

I waited for him to continue. Instead, his dark eyes bore into mine.

"What's that?" I finally asked, not knowing if I really wanted the answer or not.

"Something he found on the road," Wilson continued. "Something you're going to find interesting. And you ain't gonna like it."

I knew exactly what he was going to say, even before the words formed on his lips.

"Horse shit," we added, simultaneously.

"I know what he said." My tablemates each gave me condescending looks and went back to their meal. That pissed me off more. "Wilson saw it first hand; you can ask him when he comes back."

Daisy smiled at me, scooping Libby another small portion of diced carrots. "That's fine, sweetie. We believe you. There's just nothing you can do about it right now."

Violet glared at me from across the table. What did she want?

"This means we know they're around still," I added,

checking to see if Lettie seemed any more interested than the others did. She didn't. "Maybe they'll be back somewhere reachable in the next few weeks."

Slamming her fork on the table, Violet let loose. "Next few weeks?!" she shrieked. "You can't hardly walk to the road and back without sitting down for a rest. You've got a lot more than three weeks before you can do anything. If ever!"

I realized I needed a new approach. I had withheld some of the juicy information from Wilson's earlier report. Now was the time to let it fly.

"They killed the whole family," I said, meeting each of their gazes. "Father, Mother, Grandma and three kids."

Daisy stroked my arm. "This isn't really talk I think Libby should be hearing. Maybe later we can discuss this. After she's in bed."

I had their attention now. Even little miss teen sassy pants hadn't responded to the latest news. No, she just sat there playing with her food, her eyes fixated on her plate.

Lettie nodded at Daisy's suggestion. Good, we finally had a late night topic everyone would be interested in.

"Just don't get any strange ideas that you're going to run off after these creeps," Violet spoke first, as usual. That was fine, got the worst exaggerator over with right away.

Time for a little adult reasoning. "I can't blindly go after anyone, Violet," I countered. "I have to wait to be sure they're in one place for a while. Somewhere within a day's walk."

Lettie listened from the couch as if she didn't have any input. While I wanted to know what was on her mind, I figured not asking was one less person for me to argue with.

Next to her sat Daisy, her hand covering her mouth. Again, like too many times lately when the subject came up, her eyes were misty.

Violet approached and bumped my chest. "You're an idiot." She was always good for a couple of those every fight.

"Do we know if they've grown in numbers?" Daisy asked. "I think that's important to know."

"I agree with Daisy," Lettie added quickly. "This is already too dangerous of a situation. You need good recon before you go charging off and getting yourself killed."

Their joint confidence in me was overwhelming. I wasn't sure my ego could handle much more padding like that.

I knelt in front of Daisy and Lettie. Behind, I heard Violet pacing. "Okay, let's remember who's the threat here. The only reason I'm going after them is because I don't want to fight them on our turf. That leaves too much risk for one of you getting hurt. And that's unacceptable to me."

Daisy's eyes rose. "But what about you? It'll be three on one, or worse. What about your safety, Bob?"

Gently taking her hands, I smiled. "Sneak attack. I'll have everything planned, down to the last teeny-tiny detail. They'll never know what did them in."

"And you're only doing this for our continued safety," Violet snarked over my shoulder. "This has nothing to do with them killing Dizzy last winter?"

Well, if I were honest with them, the Dizzy card was always in play. But that's not what they needed to hear.

"I just want this over with so we can live in peace," I replied, watching Violet take a place on Daisy's left. "Once I'm healed, they need to be dealt with. They killed Dizzy, and now they've killed a family. We can't be next, right?"

Lettie sighed and nodded once. Daisy and Violet shared a glance. Finally, they nodded in agreement.

"You're still an idiot," Violet replied. "Just so you know."

Sure, Violet. As long as she agreed and didn't turn Daisy against me, I didn't care what she called me.

Day 1,066

If Nate's calendar was anywhere near accurate, I calculated it was mid- to late-July. And that made the never-ending thunderstorms out of place.

Most summers here (three thus far) had been dry. The first one, granted I was only here for August, brought more moisture than the second or third did, but nothing like this. Years two and three had been dry, bone dry as the saying goes. If Lettie had any cigarettes left, smoking outdoors would have been banned from mid-June on.

The past six days had been nothing but rain. So much rain that we had stopped joking about it on day three. Though Violet did think her 'let's build an ark' twice-daily comment was hilarious.

"I'm starting to worry about the garden," Lettie mentioned to me as I leaned against the front window, watching the rain slide off the roof.

I glanced at her causally. "I'm starting to worry we may need to move to higher ground." My joke didn't receive so much as a disgusted smirk.

Behind us, Libby broke into one of her screaming fits. *Oh*

goody, I thought. "I want to go outside!" she shrieked. "I don't care about the rain. I love the rain. I won't melt, I promise."

It would have been cute if it weren't the tenth or eleventh time we'd heard it. At that point, I was over the child, the crying baby and my housemates. Maybe even myself.

"Come on," Violet said, taking the child by the arm, "let's work on your letters." Pencil and paper sat on the table, waiting her arrival. But our little darling five-year-old had other plans.

Planting her heels, she crossed her tiny arms. "I hate school. I hate letters. I hate math. And I hate rain!"

I chuckled at her frustrated mother. "And I'm not real keen on a certain child right now myself." At least that got a smile.

We needed a break in the weather, badly.

During the night, the thunder and wind returned after a late afternoon lull. We were going to die, I feared. Either by drowning or by tornado. At least we would be done with the rain.

Resting, not sleeping, next to Daisy, I listened to an odd sound. It was hard to pick up through the wind at first, but the more I strained to listen, the clearer it became.

"What is that tapping on the roof?" Daisy asked, sitting up

on an elbow.

"Hail," I moaned. Weren't the wind and rain bad enough? Did we really need this plague too?

"What's this going to do to the garden?" Daisy gasped. "I mean, this can't be good, can it?"

I lay back down and invited Daisy to do the same by patting her pillow. "There's nothing we can do. We'll just have to wait until morning and see what the damage is."

She snuggled in close. I wrapped my free arm around her. "Okay, I guess we can wait until morning. I suppose we should get some sleep," she finally relented.

A bright flash lit the night sky, followed by a rolling drum of thunder. *Good luck with that*, I thought as I drifted to sleep.

Day 1,068

One more day of rain and the skies finally cleared. That was good; with any luck, we'd be able to walk out to the garden within a week and not sink to our knees in mud. The chances of Libby playing in the yard in the next few days weren't good. Since I'd grown used to her whine, that wasn't such a big deal anymore.

After lunch, Lettie and I meandered out the door and made our way over the soggy yard to the garden.

"Well this sucks," I said, shaking my head at the dirt. The few plants that the storm didn't destroy showed no signs of life. What the hail hadn't pummeled to lifeless stalks, the water had swept away.

Rubbing her chin, Lettie sighed. "This has happened before. Maybe not at such a precarious time, but I've seen it this bad in the past."

"Is it salvageable?" I asked, silently saying a prayer that it might be.

Lettie grinned. "Not a snowball's chance in hell."

Well, that settled that.

***

Violet and Daisy saved their judgment until sunset when they finally dared to peek at the disaster. In deep purple rain boots, Libby sledged through the rows of the former garden, her steps making a sucking sound. It was perhaps the most depressing sound I'd ever heard. Well, short of gunfire pointed in my direction.

Daisy sniffed back her emotions. "Well, this is kinda hard to swallow." Another sniff and she quickly wiped away a rogue tear. "Maybe if we replant right away, once this dies out, we could still salvage something."

I circled the plot, reaching for Libby so she wouldn't trample the few peas, or beans, or whatever they were. Violet's stance, upright with arms crossed tightly over her chest, were all I needed to see. *Why even look at her face,* I wondered. *She's not going to be happy.*

"We're going to starve to death," Violet stated in a spiteful tone. "We'll never make it through next winter. We're screwed."

She stomped away, ripping the front door open, making sure it slammed as loudly as possible. I rolled my eyes and glanced at Daisy. For her part, she seemed unaffected by Violet's tantrum.

"We'll figure this out," Daisy replied, nodding at the

garden. "We'll get through this." She looked up at me. "Let's see what Mr. Wilson has to say before we overreact."

Yeah, let's not overreact, Violet, I thought.

Day 1,075

Wilson inspected the garden with the focus of a master gardener. And as far as I knew, he was. That or a farmer extraordinaire.

Wiping his hands on his dirty jeans, he rose and approached us. The moment of truth was here.

"Deader than anything I've ever seen in my life," he said, shrugging my direction. "But I'm sure Lettie already told you that."

"Damn straight," Lettie boasted. "And this fool thinks we can try to plant again and still harvest something this fall. Talk some sense into him, Thaddeus."

Talk about being thrown under the bus. Thanks, Lettie.

His head shook. "Not enough time left to the growing season." He raised an eyebrow. "Not up here at least. Maybe 200 miles south of here you could get away with it. But here in the UP—"

I raised a hand. "I get it, Wilson. We're screwed." He nodded, Lettie nodded, and I dropped into a further state of frustration. "So what's your advice?"

He rubbed his chin for a while before taking a seat on a

nearby stump. Lettie and I strolled over to be closer to him.

"The way I see it," he drawled, "you need some help here, which is good."

I glanced at Lettie, hoping she understood what was possibly good about losing your garden for the year. Dandelion season, after all, had come and gone.

"I need help over at my place," Wilson added. "I need some expertise with my crops so we get a full harvest. I didn't get the hail, and my drainage is set up better than yours is. But I do need some expert advice to get the most out of everything."

He wanted Lettie. She was probably the best known gardener in the area. At least the best known still alive. Here she had made things grow in dirt where the grass wouldn't even take hold. Now with our garden gone, her expertise was needed elsewhere.

"What's in it for us?" I asked solemnly.

"He'll share," Lettie firmly stated. "With me there, he'll get a good harvest. A harvest that we can split between our groups, right Thaddeus?"

After a short pause, he nodded. "I mean you don't have anything else to trade me, Bob. And while I don't mind helping out, I'm not gonna feed you all winter for free."

His words were sobering. They reminded me how one wrong move could wipe out an entire family. And not just gardening.

"I'll have to tell the girls," Lettie said. "Give us a couple days and then one of your boys can haul me back to your place in a cart. I'm not walking all that ways."

Rising from the stump, I noticed his grin. "I wouldn't expect you to, Lettie. Johnny will be happy to bring you back by us." He chuckled, something he didn't do often. "Well, maybe not happy, but he'll do as I tell him to."

Lettie hobbled back to the house. Good, I needed to talk with Wilson alone. I turned to face him.

"Still no sign of the Barster bunch," he said, anticipating my question. "All is quiet in the area, except for a few stragglers here and there from Covington."

His answer seemed a little quick to me. "You'd tell me if you had news, right?" He gave me a non-committal look. "I mean, you don't have to protect me. I've got three women in that cabin trying to stop me."

"You need to do what you need to do, Bob. I can't stop you from going after them. Hell, I get it. It's just that…" His pause made me cringe.

"You can be honest with me, Wilson."

Placing a hand on my shoulder, his tired eyes narrowed. "You gotta think this through all the way. You gotta see things from the other end. They're a band of ruthless outlaws, killers. You ain't them. You got it good here."

In the middle of No Where, at the worst time in the history of the world, this lanky bald farmer thought I had it good.

"You got a woman who cares for you," he went on. "Her child adores you. Probably a better dad to her than anyone else has ever been. The girl needs you with the baby and all." He grinned. "My granddaughter that is. You go running off seeking revenge…well, the outcome is yet to be determined."

His plain honest talk made me upset. Was everyone against me?

"You wouldn't do the same?" I asked. "You wouldn't avenge your friend and protect what's yours? Your loved ones, your family?"

"First off, Dizzy was my friend. So don't go thinking you got a corner on the market for dead friends. That last attack was near me and mine. But I'm not gonna go chasing around, picking a fight on their terms."

"So you'll wait for them to attack?" He shrugged, but I continued. "You know they will eventually. They'll come after your farm."

He leaned close to me. "Then I'll kill them," he whispered, "but not a minute before. And I think that's good advice. Something for you to heed maybe."

I raised my hand and could feel my face softening. I got it, loud and clear. If I chose to go after the murdering bunch of thieves, I was going to be on my own. So be it.

Day 1,077

Lettie had been gone for almost an hour. Still the tears continued. Not that I hadn't expected them from Daisy. No, her soft heart and warm feelings made her friend's leaving difficult. She understood that it had to happen; she just couldn't hide her sadness.

As Daisy cried, so did Libby. She was what, six now? Her mother was her world. Mine too, but my wife — the one in Chicago — always said I was an emotionless person. Guess she missed the part where I spiked my coffee cup against the wall. The event that led me here, the event that stranded me here.

Daisy and Libby cried openly, sitting together on the bench outside the front door of the cabin. I gave hugs and light kisses, letting them get the sorrow out. I wasn't heartless, just non-emotional.

A little later, I held Daisy in my arms while Libby chased a butterfly in the yard. Most of the weeping was over. All that was left were the last few sniffles.

"You should go check on Vi and the baby," she said, rubbing my bare arm. "Make sure she's okay."

She was okay. The girl was tougher than a boiled owl. Her father died, no tears. Her mother left, same result. When Wilson led Nate away earlier in the summer, she never even gave it a second glance.

Poking my head inside, I couldn't find her. The cabin was small, so the task shouldn't have been hard. In the bedroom, Hope slept peacefully in the bed, pillows and blankets wrapped around her to prevent her from rolling off.

But no Violet…anywhere.

Back in the main room, I paused, wondering where the girl might be. Shrugging, I took a step for the door when I heard something from the far corner. Soft at first, but definitely the sound of crying.

I slid the shower curtain back slowly so as not to startle her. Kneeling, I gave her a small smile.

"What you doing in the shower, Violet?"

With the butt of her palm, she cleaned her cheeks. Glaring at me, her red eyes swam with tears.

"Could you give me a little privacy?" she vented.

"The place is too small for that, sweetie. We're all in this together."

Her stare intensified. "Then why aren't you crying?" she shouted.

I chuckled. "Because I'm heartless, or so some people claim. And it's the way it has to be. We'll get fed this way. It'll be better."

Her face sank to her hands and the sobbing intensified. "How can you say it'll be better? This is getting worse every single day."

Yeah, things were getting ugly. I couldn't argue with her about that. But we had enough people here to still be okay.

"We'll be fine," I replied, rubbing the top of her head.

She looked up at me; her cheeks stained with rivers of dampness. "First my dad, then Dizzy. Then Mom leaves and now Lettie. Who's next? I can't take one more person leaving me."

I opened my arms and she fell against my chest, still heaving with sobs. The girl who never needed a hug needed a hug. I tried to shush her, but she needed to let it out.

So I just let her cry.

Dinner was quiet. Somehow, Daisy knew to stay silent, just offering Violet a small smile or a pat on her hand from time to time. Libby sensed something as well and spent most of the meal on the teen's lap, hugging her. Thankfully, Hope slept soundly after her bedtime bottle.

I figured it had to be some kind of female intuition, this thing about knowing when to talk and when not to. As usual, I had no idea when was the right time for either.

"Bob, what are your plans for tomorrow?" Daisy asked in a cheery tone. "Any idea of where we stand on wood?"

We'd been almost completely silent up until now, so her question jolted me from a near fugue-like state.

"I'd like to try and cut at least four big sections tomorrow," I answered, narrowing my eyes at Daisy. She simply wiped her mouth and smiled back at me like I was missing something. Most likely I was.

"Perhaps Vi might be able to help you with that," Daisy continued, giving the teen a glance. If she did want to help, it didn't show on her face. "If you would *like* to help, Vi."

Vi gave a small nod, though I was unsure whether it meant yes or was the prelude to a major blowout.

"I could probably do that," she whispered, hugging Libby with her left arm while pushing venison around her plate with her free hand. "As long as you don't mind watching Hope?"

"I'd love to watch Hope all day," Daisy replied in her continuing upbeat way. I never would have tried this method. I feared for my life more than that. But Daisy somehow knew best. She always did.

Another pregnant pause followed, interrupted by the occasional clink of silverware on a plate or a water glass being thumped on the table.

"Do you think Lettie's ever coming back?" Violet asked in a depressed tone.

Daisy grabbed her hand in hers. "Yes, she is. She'll be back after the fall harvest. You can set your watch by it." She grinned broadly and I finally saw the first hint of a smile from Violet all day. "That is, if we had watches anymore."

Even I managed a smile with her lighthearted approach. Things were going to be quiet without Lettie, but we were going to be okay.

Day 1,088

She chucked a piece of wood in my direction. "If you were able to split a piece of wood in a decent fashion, maybe the pile out back wouldn't keep tipping over." Violet stormed away, stomping as hard as she could on the brown sandy soil.

I watched her until she rounded the corner of the cabin. "You almost hit me!" I shouted. Truth was she hadn't come close, but I figured it was my turn to cast dispersions. She certainly had tossed enough of them at me over the past few weeks.

Working with Violet, helping her get over her depression, wasn't improving my mood. I thought I'd witnessed all of her worst episodes throughout the past three years, until we tried to do this chore together.

The worst had been when she begged to use the ax and then damn near chopped my foot off. As much as I tried to remain calm, it became impossible. Mostly because she felt her actions were inevitably somehow my fault.

Daisy trotted between us most days, Hope pulled tight against her. She was mostly afraid that I was going to kill Violet, which was a very real possibility. What she said over and over — and over — to Violet, I didn't care. As far as I was concerned, they could have been plotting against me, and that was fine with me. At least it would release me from the hell I'd been trapped in since Lettie left.

Two days prior, Wilson showed up, all smiles. That was odd for a man I wasn't sure even had teeth until he showed proof. Seemed that Lettie was a godsend. His crops had already improved, all due to the old gal's magic touch. And of course, that pissed Violet off.

Everything, in all reality, pissed the girl off. If I was happy and whistling a tune, she was mad. If I didn't smile and perhaps didn't answer a request quickly enough, she was mad. If I paid too much attention to Libby, if I dared to hug Daisy, if I made goo-goo eyes at Hope, the girl was mad.

And I was perpetually confused.

I didn't care about the feelings of an almost 15 year old, if I was honest about it. Her mood changed a little more frequently than the hourly temperature. Her and her mood swings weren't my problem.

Or so I thought.

Daisy and I sat on the bench, enjoying the last of the sunshine just before the mosquitoes came out for their nightly feast.

When I went to hold her hand, she checked to make sure Violet was busy inside.

I grinned at her and she looked confused.

"Can we just kill her?" I asked, smiling for the first time all day.

Daisy laid her head on my shoulder. "It's hard being a teenaged girl, and a mother, and living like this."

I shook my head. "Yeah, and it's a real blast living with a teenager, who's a mother, in the middle of the apocalypse. Such a delight."

"She feels abandoned, Bob. People she loves and cares about are either gone or dead. You have to remember that, please."

Yeah, and once upon a time I was going to try to get back to my wife, I thought, but decided to leave that out.

"So why's she always pissed at me?" I asked, glancing around to make sure the demon teen wasn't listening.

Daisy gave me a quizzical look, as if she didn't understand the question.

"You know better. Don't be dense," she answered, crossing her arms and turning away.

"I have no idea what you're talking about, Daisy. Really."

"You want to run off and fight Clyde Barster," she replied

in a quiet voice. "She's scared she'll lose you, too. Don't pretend like you don't know that."

I could tell from Daisy's voice that Violet wasn't the only one worried about losing me.

"I don't have any idea where he or his gang is right now, Daisy." My retort probably sounded fairly pissy, but I didn't care. "No one's losing me anytime soon. Unless I die from boredom or an ax to the head from you-know-who."

Daisy laughed. "Vi cares about you far too much to ever hurt you."

Maybe, maybe not.

Day 1,090

Another day in paradise, chopping wood with a teen seething with enough vitriol to fill an Olympic-sized swimming pool. How much fun was one guy allowed? Worst of all, I had no way of escaping her wrath, though I tried often.

Earlier in the morning, I had snuck out before anyone was awake. I enjoyed the orange glow of the sunrise, the smell of the pines and morning dew on the grass, the sounds of birds calling to one another, lost in a forest of multiple shades of green foliage that enveloped our home.

My goal was to re-stack the wood that kept tipping over behind the cabin. Truth be told, the last year's cuttings didn't look too well organized on the south side either. But my cutting wasn't the cause of the issue. No, it was my helper.

An hour or so into my work, I sensed an exasperated, unpleasant presence behind me. It had to be *her*.

"Why do you despise me so badly?" Violet spewed. "Why didn't you wake me so I could explain to you what I had done back here? Why do you insist on sneaking around, pretending you're the only one here?"

Unhappy with the early morning ambush, I spun on my

heels and glared at her. "Well good morning, sunshine! Did you sleep well?"

Her arms were tightly crossed over her chest, eyes narrowed and focused on me. "What don't you get? The part where I'm trying to help you? Or maybe that I'm not the enemy, but rather your friend?"

Wow, she must have been awake for hours dreaming up that rant. "I had friends, once upon a time. But none of them seemed to hate me as badly as you do." I took a deep breath, trying to hold back my own personal tirade. *Screw it*, I decided. *She needed an attitude adjustment.*

"You know, Violet, if you don't like something, I wish you'd just spit it out. If you hate me so much, get it out. Tell me why. But if you're just being a pissy teenager, then grow up. I don't have time for your bullshit."

She drummed her fingers against her arm, her eyes locked on mine. If she was going to let loose with any tears, she didn't let on.

"You don't get it. You'll never get it," she replied, a little less angry.

"Try me. You might find I'm fairly open-minded."

She opened her mouth to speak, but I cut her off.

"If this," I said, stepping closer, "if any of this is about me going after Barster, you can just forget it. I'm not flexible on the subject."

She nodded once and stepped closer, right up to me. Raising her shaky hands, she placed one on each side of my face. Perching on her tiptoes, she was coming far too close for my comfort. But I refused to budge, refused to back down. If she wanted my attention that badly to get that close and let me have it, then I'd let her have it her way.

What she did next shocked the absolute living shit out of me.

There, behind the cabin, next to the woodpile, in a spot I was fairly certain no one inside could see, she kissed me. And it wasn't a quick peck on the cheek. It was on the lips and hard, with a velvet tinge of passion. It wasn't what a sister would give a brother. Oh no, there was nothing platonic about it.

And for a fleeting moment, ever so briefly, I enjoyed it.

Quickly I forced myself back to my senses, but the damage had already been done. Her confused feelings about me were now out in the open.

But I was an adult, she a mere child — at least what I considered a child.

"What the hell is wrong with you?" I whispered angrily when I'd finally separated us to a comfortable distance.

She shook her head slightly. "You're what's wrong with me."

Like that helped. Three seconds earlier, I seemed to be the solution, not the problem.

Reaching out, she stroked my arm. "I'm so alone. I can't tell you, I can't tell Daisy, I couldn't talk to Mom or Lettie. I don't know what to do. I'm so scared Daisy is going to see through my façade and then I'll lose her, too. I don't know what to do, Bob. I'm so scared."

"You're 15, Violet. I'm 27…or 28. Whichever. This isn't allowed in our society."

That's when the tears started. I had to give her credit for holding them back so long.

"What society?" she asked, laughing. "And who cares about age? I'm a woman, I'm a mother, and I've had to grow up so much in the past three years. I'm not a child anymore, if that's how you see me."

I focused on her closely. "I never said you were a child. I know you've been through a lot. But there's this thing between Daisy and I. And you know it exists. You see it every day."

Violet wiped away several tears. "Sometimes I wished she'd

leave," she whispered, eyes cast to the ground. "And that only makes me feel worse. She's so good to me. She helps with Hope, even when I don't ask her to. But most of the time, I wish she wasn't here, and it was just you, me and Hope."

My head spun out of control. Never had I dreamt *this* was the source of our tension.

"It would never work, Violet. You need someone your own age... like Jimmy Wilson."

She scoffed at the suggestion with a grunt.

"And Daisy's not going anywhere. You know that. And if she finds out how you feel, I don't know how she would react." I thought I saw her expression shift, more accepting almost, but it was hard to tell.

She gazed at me, her eyes larger than I'd ever seen before. "Do you love me?"

Holy shit this was getting serious. I knew I had to say something a little better than *'you're crazy.'*

I took her hand and smiled. "I love you, I love Daisy. I love Libby, and Hope, and Lettie. You're all my family. How could I possibly not love any of you?"

I figured it was the gentlest way of letting her down. I was always stupid, and that moment was no different.

"Can you just tell me that every once in a while?" she

begged. "You don't have to mean it, but just hearing it will make this all more bearable."

"You know how I really feel, Violet. My heart is pure, and it belongs to Daisy."

She nodded and then leaned in for a hug. That seemed like the least I could do for her. She'd been brutally honest with me and probably didn't get the result she had hoped for.

"I love you," she whispered. I thought about reminding her of what I just said, but she looked up and caught me off guard. "And I know Daisy has never told you that."

Damn it. She was slyer than I'd thought. Maybe the hug, the one she was still clutching tightly, hadn't been my best idea.

I opened my mouth to warn her off, but a scream from the front of the cabin cut me off. A long, mournful scream that was becoming hysterical by the second.

"Daisy!" Violet and I uttered at the same time, running as fast as we could to the house.

Day 1,090 - continued

I beat Violet to the porch to find Daisy crying and pointing towards the road. I expected to see visitors on horseback. However, a careful study of the blacktop revealed nothing.

"What is it?" I gasped, out of breath from my short sprint. "What is it, Daisy?"

She pointed, and behind us, Violet let out a stillness-shattering scream. My head tore around to face her, only to see the same look of horror on her face, crying and pointing, unable to make out words.

I looked towards the road again, taking a few steps towards it. Everything was calm, all was quiet, and nothing was out of place.

I turned back to them. "I don't see anything. What am I missing?"

They both continued to sob and scream and point. Libby came out the front door.

"On the other side of the road," Daisy sobbed, "in the trees, just right of the dead spruce."

I looked again, but still saw nothing. Maybe a few crows, but nothing life-threatening.

Just before I turned around again, I saw a crow land on something. That was when Libby let loose with a scream of her own.

I took a few more steps forward and stopped, feeling my body shudder.

On the far side of the road, right where Daisy said, hung two charred bodies. Ropes were wrapped around their hands, feet and necks. The crow pecked at the blackened flesh.

With no one's help, I cut the bodies down from the tree. Except for the smell of charred flesh, the task wasn't as bad as I thought it would be. It was dead people, and it was all gruesome and such, but the screaming women were worse in my mind.

From across the road, Violet shouted instructions, "Are they real? You should bury them. If they're not real, you don't have to, I guess. If you need help, you'll have to wait until Mr. Wilson comes tomorrow. I'm not helping and Daisy says she's physically ill because of all of this. Don't you think you should catch them instead of letting them drop like that?"

That was it. I trotted across the road to the cowering teen.

"Listen, this is bad enough without all the commentary," I hissed. "And of course they're real people." She looked at me funny. "Well, they *were* real people. Now, they're just dead people."

She peered around me at the stiffies. "Are they burnt?" She clutched at my arm. "Like burnt to death?"

I gazed back across the road. "I don't know if they were fried pre- or post-mortem. But that's really not the worst part."

She looked at me, horrified. "How could it possibly be any worse?"

"You don't want to know the details, trust me."

"Tell me, Bob. I deserve to know."

I gave her a sideways glance. "Well, they're naked, of course. Their eyes have been gouged out, and they seem to be missing most of their front teeth." I heard her gasp, but there was more. "Neither has a tongue, the man's, um...thing has been cut off, and unless I'm mistaken, women are supposed to have breasts."

Her eyes stared off into the distance, opened wide as dinner plates. "Who did this?"

I handed her something I'd found nailed to the man's back. A single piece of white paper that looked so out of place that there was no missing it.

She read it aloud, "Leaf now." I noticed her head shake.

"So, we know they're illiterate." Violet nodded. "But aside from that, I've got no idea who sent this message."

Violet continued to study the note. "It all seems kind of extreme to me."

"No shit, sunshine. I think that was the point of it all. Shock and awe, you know."

She looked at me confused. "I don't follow."

"You know, George Bush, Iraq, shock and awe."

She shrugged. "I don't remember that, I guess. And what does any of this have to do with dead people?"

I pushed past and wondered where I'd put my shovel. "Are you going to help me bury them or what?"

I peeked back to find her still staring across the road at the bodies.

"I think I hear Hope crying," she muttered, turning for the cabin.

Some help she was. At least we were off the subject from earlier. Maybe that was all behind us now.

Day 1,091

Wilson showed up the day after I expected him. Either I had the day wrong or Wilson was on his own schedule. Either option was plausible.

After hearing the story three times, once from each of us, mine less hysterical than theirs, he walked across the road with me and studied the crime scene.

"Any ideas?" I asked, watching him kick at the brown weeds beneath the hanging tree.

He moved slowly through the underbrush. "Yeah," Wilson drawled, "someone wants you to leave. Wants your place, probably your supplies, too."

That part bothered me. Any outsider who thought we were living high on the hog was sadly mistaken.

Our meals consisted of stewed meats — beef, pork, chicken, venison — a small smattering of vegetables, a limited number of ugly potatoes and burnt flat bread. We rarely drank anything other than well water, and even that wasn't a treat anymore due to the brown color that infiltrated it each summer.

"They don't know what they're asking for," I ruminated,

watching my friend continue his search. "I don't think anyone lives very well anymore. Anywhere."

He looked back at me with a crooked half-smile. "If they got nothing, or next to nothing, it probably looks to them like you're living in the lap of luxury. If they've seen me bringing you supplies, they know you got something. And that sure beats the hell out of having nothing."

Wilson emerged from the brush, picking a wood tick off his arm and casting it aside. "Let's check the road."

We walked a mile south, then another just for good measure. I checked in with my family before we made the same trek north. According to Daisy, they were fine. They still had Lettie's 30-30 next to the door, ready for action if needed. Violet begged me not to leave again. The hour absence made her anxious, she claimed. Daisy helped sooth her nerves as Wilson and I headed north.

I had checked the road in both directions the afternoon after finding the burnt corpses. Though I had only traveled several hundred yards in each direction, I found nothing. At least that day.

All the way to the first bend, some 200 yards, was clean. That wasn't news to me. However, shortly after the bend clues began to pop up. Easy clues to spot.

Almost four years of the apocalypse had left the roads barren. Here and there the blacktop crumbled. In some spots it was almost gone, revealing the gravel beneath the formerly jet-black surface.

Branches and leaves were the only things on the road, and those were more prevalent in the fall and spring. During the summer, the winds and rains cleansed the roads of debris. That's what made the mess ahead so noticeable.

Wilson kicked at the pile in the middle of the road. "Looks like this is two, maybe three days old." He peered ahead, further up the road. "Looks like another pile a little ways up."

I was glad he was a horseshit expert. The timing spoke volumes.

"So, most likely the Barster gang?" I looked back at him for confirmation, getting a non-committal shrug.

"They're probably not the only people with horses up here, but could be, I suppose."

His tone was less than convincing and his posture made me wonder what he was thinking.

"Can you find out if they're back in the area?" I asked as he kneeled down in the gravel. "Just so we know. I think it's important for both of us to be clear on this."

His lips slid from side to side over his brown stained teeth. He stroked his beard several times before removing his hat. Wiping his head with a dirty brown rag, he rose.

"This may not be a war you can win, Bob," he replied, his eyes as tight as his dry lips. "You may want to consider all your options. They could have recruited reinforcements."

I felt the blood rush to my extremities. Did he really think there was a world where I wouldn't go after the people who had killed my friend? The hoodlums who had terrorized us not once, not twice, but at least three times? If he did, he was sorely mistaken.

"There's two options," I whispered, peering back down the road towards my place. "One, I hunt them down. Two, I wait them out and kill them when they show up again." I turned and faced Wilson head on. "Either way, they're leaving this Earth in a gruesome fashion."

His face hardened. "More gruesome than burning and mutilating people? I'm not sure you have that in you."

I nodded slightly. "You'd be surprised what I'd do to protect my family, Wilson. Mighty surprised."

Day 1,092

We argued amongst ourselves for a day and a half. But nothing, nor no one, was about to change my mind.

After dinner, we sat around the table. Both Libby and Hope slept soundly in the bedroom. Violet had left the door slightly ajar in case the baby awoke.

"Here's what I think," Daisy began, reaching for my hands. I was sure I wasn't going to like whatever she had to say. "Maybe we need to go and move in with Mr. Wilson, like he suggested. It sounds like he has enough room for us all. And it would be much safer."

I opened my mouth to counter, but Violet beat me to it.

"I can't move in there," Violet stated, pursing her lips. "I can't. And you know why, Daisy."

Daisy nodded and smiled at her. "But this may be necessary for our survival, Vi. For Hope's survival as well. You see that, don't you?"

Violet shook her head fiercely. "I can't. He's never come to see me or Hope. And I don't even want to see him again. Please don't make me."

I placed a hand in each of their directions. "There's a

bigger issue than just moving in with Jimmy Wilson. It's all about survival. Moving locations will probably just put off the pending battle. It's not going away."

Daisy looked at me with pleading eyes. "There has to be some other solution, Bob. There just has to be."

I folded my arms across my chest. "We stand and fight, or I hunt them down. This has to be taken care of now. We can't wait one more year, even one more season. You saw what they did to those people they left hanging across the road. The time is now."

Violet ran her fingers through her hair, tugging at the ends. "I agree," she whispered, a bit of vibrato caught in her words. "I think you should take Jimmy and Johnny and go take care of this. That's what I think."

Daisy's jaw dropped, her head shaking back and forth. "No, please. I don't want anything to happen to you or the Wilson boys. We need to seek refuge with them. Together we'll make our stand. Even Mr. Wilson said that was a good idea."

The tides had changed, and Daisy knew it. It was always me against them, but now I had Violet standing firmly in my corner.

"I won't give up this place," I retorted. "They drove us from Lettie's. They're not driving us out of here."

Daisy turned to me, clutching my hands in hers. "Bob, I don't want anything to happen to you. I don't think I can live without you. You have to know that."

"I can't either," Violet added quietly. Her eyes met ours. "But I can't live in fear anymore. Most nights I lie out here awake, listening for you at the window, Bob. If I think you've fallen asleep, I lift my head to make sure your eyes are still open. And when you take guard Daisy, I don't sleep at all. We can't keep going like this. It's not fair to any of us."

Daisy swiped away a few stray tears streaking down her tanned cheek. "I've just been hoping and praying it wouldn't come to this. I just thought that maybe they'd move on. I don't want anything to happen to any of us. That's all I care about — our safety."

I rose and walked over to the front window. "Wilson will be back when he has news. Either that, or he'll be back in four days with more supplies. Something tells me that before summer is over, this is coming to a head."

Violet and Daisy exchanged a look. "How long until the end of summer?" Violet asked.

"Probably a month," I answered, gazing at the twilight outside. "I figure its mid-August. Another month before it starts to turn into fall. If we don't do something before then, they'll be here to visit us."

"Maybe something good will come before then," Daisy said, a tinge of hope back in her voice. "Perhaps they'll lose interest in us and move on. Or maybe they'll meet some other demise and never make it back." She smiled at me and the frowning Violet. "I can just feel it in my bones, Vi. This will resolve itself without any violence on our part."

Violet rubbed the top of Daisy's extended hand. "Or maybe Bob will go after them and get this over with so we can live in peace."

Daisy's face fell. They weren't the words she wanted to hear, and were probably closer to the truth than she wanted to admit.

Day 1,095

Each day we waited for word from Wilson. I knew the Barster gang had to be back in the area. It was only a matter of time before he showed up. I used the quiet time to prepare myself.

And each day we steadfastly watched the road, always on guard for some type of sneak attack. My pistol never left my side, even when I went to the outhouse. Lettie's old 30-30 sat propped next to the door, ready for action if need be.

Daisy finally gave in to the idea of me going after them before they came for us. I'm not sure if it was the pressure of the situation, or maybe it was one of the whispered conferences I heard Daisy and Violet having late at night. Or perhaps it was when Violet changed her vote, and Daisy knew she was outnumbered.

Whatever the reason, we all finally agreed.

Anytime I noticed any movement on the road, or anywhere for that matter, a knot formed in the pit of my stomach. At first, I drew my weapon every time a twig snapped or a squirrel chased another through the woods. I found myself flinching at every sound, every strange sight.

I knew hunting down Barster could lead to my eventual

demise, but I had to do it, and however it happened, it needed to be soon. If for no other reason, we needed a release from the constant tension that filled our days.

I heard the screen door close and then footsteps. Someone was coming to visit me while I took an extended break from chopping wood. I felt a hand take mine, small delicate fingers intertwining my rough calloused digits.

"Daisy," I said with a smile.

"Close, but you only had two choices." I jumped back at the sound of Violet's voice. *What was she up to now*, I wondered.

"Don't worry, she fell asleep putting Libby and Hope down for their nap," Violet said, pointing at the house. "The curtains are even drawn. She won't see us."

Circling a log to get a few extra steps away, I studied her skeptically. "She won't see us because nothing we're going to be doing is worth seeing," I said firmly. There, now she knew where we stood.

She crossed her arms, staring into the woods. "You know, when you kissed me last week, I noticed you let it linger an extra moment."

I felt my eyes bug open. "You kissed me!" I countered in a hushed whisper.

She looked back at me and rolled her eyes. "Whatever,

Romeo. You just didn't seem too hasty to end our lip lock."

"Violet," I said, as evenly as possible, peering through the front window. I needed to be sure Daisy wasn't standing there, listening in on something she might misconstrue. "You're 15 years old. As delightful as you may think—"

"I'm 18," she countered.

I felt my eyes narrow. "Three falls ago you said you were 12. This next spring will be the third one since whatever went wrong. That makes you 15 now, and 16 in the spring."

A sly smile curled the corners of her lips. "And you were the only one whoever bought that story."

"What?"

She took a step closer. "Mom thought I'd be less attractive, and safer, if we told people I was 12, that way we wouldn't have a bunch of men like you perving on me all the time. Because I looked so young, she knew people would believe it. At least she hoped they would."

She took another step closer and I became a little uncomfortable. "Dizzy never believed it; he saw right through it somehow. Lettie laughed the first time Mom told her. She said I didn't have the hips of a 12 year old. Daisy never could remember what age we agreed upon for our little fib. Not that you ever noticed."

She grinned, pointing a finger at me. "But you bought it. Hook..." she took another step closer, "...line..." another step and she was next to me, taking my hand. "...and sinker." She raised it to her mouth and kissed it.

"I don't believe you." I actually wasn't sure, but the confusion pulsing through my brain made it hard to think clearly.

"I'll be 19 next spring. All of a sudden I'm not so young anymore, am I, Mr. Reiniger?"

She still had my hand in hers. I tugged it away. Lord only knew where it could have ended up next.

"It doesn't change a thing, Violet. Daisy and I are a couple. And you know that." I stepped away and picked up my ax. "Now, why don't you fill the water buckets for tonight, as long as everyone else is napping."

She turned, flipping her brown hair over her shoulder. "Okay, play hard to get. I can wait." She skipped several paces before stopping and turning. "But remember, I love you. I said it first. And I'm the only one thus far. But you knew that, right?"

I watched her scoop the bucket off the stump by the corner of the house before disappearing into the woods. *What the hell is she up to?* I pondered in stunned confusion. Well *good luck, little girl. I'm not interested.*

We ate another evening meal in silence. While I exchanged smiles with Daisy, I caught Violet staring at us…or perhaps it was just me. She was going to ruin my life if she wasn't careful.

"No Mr. Wilson again today," Daisy said, causing me to jump. "He should be here tomorrow or the next day with some more food."

Violet forked a green bean and lifted it to her nose, sniffing it suspiciously. "Yep," she replied, stuffing it into her mouth.

Beside Daisy, Libby chomped on a piece of dried venison. "I hope Grandpa Wilson brings us something decent to eat this time," she complained. "I didn't like his last delivery."

Daisy turned and stroked the top of her daughter's head. "We mustn't complain about free food, Libby. Grandpa Wilson has been very good to us."

Setting her fork on the table, Libby stared at her mother. "But he took Grandma Lettie."

"We traded Grandma for some food," Violet inserted, grinning at me. "Not a very good trade, based on what we've received lately."

"It only has been a few weeks," Daisy countered, eyeing

Violet casually. "You can't expect Lettie to perform miracles overnight, can you Vi?"

"It's been three weeks, and it wasn't a fair trade," Violet snarked.

Damn that child, or teen, or whatever she was. Now she was picking fights with her only female friend left within five miles. I had no idea what her latest ploy was, but it seemed foolish to me.

"Bob, what do you think?" Daisy asked, catching me off guard. A smile flashed across Violet's face. Damn it, she needed to stop this game.

"Lettie had to go, Violet," I answered. Her eyes narrowed with anger. "Otherwise we'd starve to death. You know that."

She rose from her spot, pointing a fork at me. "You'd agree with anything Daisy told you to. Why don't you grow a spine?" Tossing her fork onto the table, she ran to the bedroom and slammed the door. Hope began screaming.

"Oh no," Daisy fretted, getting up from her spot, "now the baby's awake. Oh, poor Vi will be all in a tizzy now. Can you clean up while I help her, sweetie?"

I nodded, piling plates on top of one another. "Sure, no problem."

"Oh, and Bob?" Daisy whispered. "Maybe you could be a

little sweeter to Vi, please? She looks up to you so, and I really think she could use a kind word or two from you. You know how she thinks you walk on water."

The bedroom door creaked open and Hope's cries intensified. When the door closed, I heard Daisy's sweet voice singing a lullaby. I listened closely to see if the two women said anything to one another.

Not only was Violet playing me like a cheap guitar, she was warming up on Daisy as well.

Day 1,097

Two days later, Wilson arrived during a drizzle. In one hand, he carried a large goody bag of supplies. In the other was a small satchel, most likely containing clothes. I spied him coming through the front window with Daisy at my side. Once she realized he was coming to stay, she left in tears, running into the bedroom with Violet.

My breath caught a little and I felt a slight chill run through my veins. I was really going to do this, I thought. For a fleeting moment, before Wilson reached our front door, I doubted myself.

I studied myself in the mirror. "You could die," I whispered to the ghost of my former self. A man no longer recognizable in my eyes, a man shot and left for dead twice, a man who had taken the lives of others.

I listened to the sounds coming from the bedroom. Violet and Libby were comforting Daisy, begging her to dry her tears. Daisy's sniffles saying it was all right. Hope cooing, Libby was probably entertaining her.

"If you don't do this, they're all dead within a month," I warned my mirrored self.

Wilson was a dozen steps from the front door. I took a deep breath and pulled up my loose pants.

It was show time.

Day 1,097 — continued

As if it were a special occasion, we sipped tea like civilized people. But it wasn't a special occasion, not for me. I'd said I'd make coffee. Wilson claimed that sounded fine.

The bedroom door flung open and Daisy appeared with red swollen eyes, a broad smile and a plan.

So, we had tea.

Daisy brought out tiny floral cups and saucers I'd scavenged somewhere for her, though I couldn't recall any longer where or even when I had found them. After the water boiled long enough for her liking, she and Violet seeped the teabags in a matching floral pot. I hated it when they plotted together. Nothing good ever came of it.

Blowing on his tea, Wilson shot me a crooked smile. I couldn't blame him. The hot beverage tasted like dirt, and the cups looked out of place in our large calloused hands. I decided to bite my tongue for a bit just to humor Daisy. But I didn't plan on this being a long farewell party.

"So, Mr. Wilson," Daisy started, trying to smile and hold back sniffles and tears. "Tell me and Vi all about how Lettie is doing. We're just bursting for news."

I noticed his eyes flash my way before he gave the gals a decent smile. Well decent enough for a man whose idea of a smile looked like he was passing bad gas.

"She's good," he answered. "Doing well."

Daisy nodded. "And the garden? Has she been able to help?"

Wilson eased a bit. "Oh yeah, everything looks a lot better already. That old gal knows all the tricks."

Violet cleared her throat. "And how are your sons?" she asked.

I'm sure my mouth dropped obscenely open with her question. Like she gave a damn about how Jimmy or Johnny were doing.

"Something wrong, Bob?" Violet scolded. Damn it, busted.

I shook my head in a small way. "No." I figured the pending fight could wait a few minutes. Daisy's smile helped quell my growing anger, though Violet's pissy expression made my anger want to boil over. Daisy won…for now.

"Boys are fine," Wilson answered. "Work hard and eat like mules." He let out a snort/laugh. "So that's good, I guess."

"And Nate?" Violet continued. "How's my brother?"

"Ha!" I couldn't help it. The questions were getting more and more ridiculous.

Violet's eyes bored into mine. "If there's a problem, Bob, perhaps we can discuss it later."

I thought about shrugging, but decided it was my turn to speak.

"Like you give a rat's ass about Nate," I raged. "You've never asked about him once in all this time. Spare me the show."

Daisy placed her hand gently on my arm. "Please try and be gentle with Vi's feelings," she said in a soft voice. "She's worried about Nate."

I turned to face her and shook my head. "She's stalling. You're both stalling. I know what you're doing. Just so we're square on that."

Giving me another of her patented smiles, Daisy acted as if she had no idea what I was talking about. But I knew better.

"We're going to be civilized," Violet shrieked from across the table. "Before you go off and get slaughtered, we're going to behave like decent people one last time." She leapt from her chair. "You owe us that much you son of a bitch!"

I held back a grin. She and her co-conspirator were busted and they both knew it.

"Vi," Daisy replied quietly, "we talked about this. We aren't going to get upset or show improper emotion. Please, sit down and let's continue our conversation with Mr. Wilson and Bob."

Glaring at me like never before — and that said a lot — Violet straightened her thin blue sleeveless shirt and retook her spot.

"Now, where were we?" Daisy asked as if nothing had happened. "I believe Vi was asking about her brother. Is he well, Mr. Wilson?"

Tightlipped and bug-eyed, Wilson studied our group perplexedly. And who could blame him? We were one happy dysfunctional family unit.

"Yep," he answered without emotion, "Nate's doing just fine. Fits in well with my boys. He's a good worker."

Daisy and Violet smiled. I rolled my eyes, crossed my arms and leaned back in my chair. This was going to take a while.

I gave it another half hour before pushing the small talk aside. One more mention of weather, crops or kids, and I would have screamed.

"They're back in the area, aren't they?" I asked, sliding my chair a little closer to Wilson's.

His lips tightened as he watched Daisy and Violet leave the table to take care of their respective children.

"Yep," he answered just above a whisper. "But I can't tell

you their exact location. Just the area I know they're in."

That was good enough for me. As long as I had a general idea and could track them down in a day or two, that was all that mattered. Yeah, it would have been better knowing the precise spot they were holed up in, but I'd waited long enough.

"So, where they at?" I asked, noting Daisy listening in on our conversation.

"Get me a piece of paper and a pencil. I can draw you a map of the area. Can't walk you right up to their front door, but I can get you close."

I rose and rifled through a pile of clutter on an end table. I knew we had clean paper somewhere in this small place.

Peeking at Violet, I dared a question. "We got any pencils or pens left around here?" She was the one who drew most of the time with Libby and helped her practice her letters.

I saw a slight grin curl the corners of her lips.

Now what?

Day 1,097 — continued

Wilson gave me a strange look as I passed his choice of writing devices across the table. He probably thought we were all a bunch of loons. He might've been right.

I smiled at him. "You have your choice of colors: black, blue, green, purple or orange."

"Crayons," he said, as if they were diseased or something.

Violet leaned over his shoulder. "You should use magenta. It's Libby's favorite."

He shook his head either at me or Violet, or perhaps both. "I'm not sure I even know what color that is…" If nothing else, he was playing along nicely.

Pencils and pens had disappeared from our home. I couldn't recall the last time I'd seen one, though I knew for a fact Libby had been practicing her letters with a pencil not long ago. Or maybe it was a crayon? Last winter, we all sat around for days coloring Christmas trees with the young girl. Thus, I just assumed everyone used crayons nowadays.

Violet handed Wilson the magenta crayon. As she pulled away, he reached for her hand and held it, giving her a kind smile.

"That Hope sure is getting big," he said. "How old is she now?"

"Almost six months," Violet answered, seeming more at ease with him than on previous visits.

"I bet she's gonna grow up to be a beautiful young lady someday, just like her mother." I swear I saw Wilson's tired eyes grow misty.

He gently let go of Violet's hand and turned to face me head on.

"These places are all just south of Covington," he began. "Probably seven miles north of here. Not the spots they were before, which were closer."

Giving him my full attention, I nodded.

"And they're a little more remote than the last place I knew they were at," Wilson continued. He lined the paper up in front of himself.

"So here's that river that crosses between Lettie's old place and town." He drew a horizontal line across the bottom of the paper. "Here's the highway." A vertical line shot up from the previous one. "And town is just off the top of the paper."

I nodded several times. "I got it." Well, sort of.

There were so many little rivers and creeks in this place it was hard to know which was which. Hopefully with a little more detail, I'd be zeroed in somewhere near my target.

Next, he drew some circles to the left of the road. That was west, at least I knew that much. However, the circles were far apart. Potential problem, I thought.

"These are the four known locations that are available to them," Wilson said, tapping the crayon in the middle of the cluster. He must have seen my concern. "Problem?"

"Yeah," I admitted. "Four spots, miles from here, and they seem a little spread out to me."

He sighed, crossing his arms. "They're all at least three miles off the main road. The furthest one might be five." His eyes met mine. "This fellow is careful. Not like he's going to set up shop right on the highway for everyone to notice. It's gonna take some craftiness to get to him."

I let out a long sigh. For the first time since I'd been planning my revenge, I wondered if it wasn't as Lettie called it — a fool's errand.

With the details laid out in front of me, I contemplated my hunt. Wilson had taken a good long time describing as much as he knew. What each of the cabins were like, what he knew about the local terrain, recent movements of the gang and what others had noticed about their fire power.

Mysteriously absent were any comments on my likelihood of winning the battle.

"You're going up against at least three people, Bob," he said, working on a plate of venison and potatoes Daisy had prepared for us. Across the table, Violet and Libby picked at their plates. Great, now the two older ones had the little girl depressed.

I contemplated my path and actions while chewing on my dinner. "Twelve miles will take most of a day. At least, if I want to move unnoticed. That's two days for a round trip." That was more than I had planned for travel time alone. Hell, I thought the whole adventure would only take two days.

"And then you gotta find them," Wilson added. "They may or may not be exactly where you expect them. I'd start with the closest place and work my way out. But that's just me."

"And we don't know if they've picked up a fourth for sure?"

He shook his head, his lips pressed together in a thin line. "Jimmy heard from a man that there were four. Another friend told me he's sure there's only three. So you'd better plan on four."

That was problematic. My goal was to catch at least two of them in the open somehow. The first would die, completely caught off guard by my attack. I could take the second as they sought cover. I hoped that the third would hole up and I could either wait them out or burn the place down around them.

A potential fourth person made the task more challenging. It allowed them to have a planned synchronized counterattack against me. And if they had enough time, or higher ground, or any other number of factors to their advantage, that could be the end of me.

"And one of them is a woman," Wilson said, picking at his teeth. "I don't know how you feel about killing a woman. That'd be hard for me."

I felt myself stiffen. "They robbed us at gunpoint, they attacked Lettie's place, they killed Dizzy. They hung two bodies out front to scare us off. I bet that same woman has been with them the whole time."

He nodded.

"Then she has it coming," I continued. "Just like Barster and anyone else left in his gang." I glanced over at Daisy as tears welled in her eyes. "An eye for an eye."

Day 1,100

I assembled my gear one day and went through the plan the next. That and rain were the only things delaying my leaving. By the morning of the third day, a light drizzle replaced the on again-off again thunderstorms. Drizzle and fog, the perfect setting to match my mood.

Daisy followed me around as I laid my gear out on the covered picnic table that Wilson and I had found several abandoned houses away. Every few minutes, she'd hug me or stop me and sneak a kiss. And every few minutes, I gave her a soft smile and went back to my preparation.

The weather and Daisy's actions made this all feel wrong. But my gut told me everything was right, and the time was now.

Wilson approached from the cabin. "One thing you got going for you is that all four places are close to the same stream. They have to have fresh water nearby. Like I told you before, you follow that same stream and you'll find all four potential hideouts."

Yeah, along with a dozen other local cabins he'd also warned me about. But I had the descriptions of the places written down, in crayon no less.

"You find them," he warned, keeping his voice low, "and then get yourself organized. Don't go charging in not knowing what the scoop is."

I nodded to myself mostly, packing the last of my provisions. I had four days of rationed food, two half-gallons of fresh water, a book of matches, an extra box of 45-caliber handgun ammo (along with a fully loaded clip already in the gun), a small tarp and a blanket. I knew I was cutting it close on food, but any extra would have weighed me down. As for the water, well that was something that was plentiful up here. As long as I didn't get mixed up with any brackish water, I'd be fine.

Daisy came up to me, tears streaming down her face again. I would have said it was getting old, but my mortality warned me to keep that thought to myself.

"Please take this with you," she said, handing me a folded piece of material. "It's a scarf I haven't worn in a while. Maybe wrap it around your neck at night so you'll think of me."

I stuffed the thin flowered material into my back pocket and leaned down to kiss her. "I'm coming back you know. Don't give up on me."

She played with the buttons of my shirt, nodding nervously and avoiding my gaze. "I know. I know."

I gave her a hug and looked inside. "I need to get going before it gets too late. I want to be off the road and somewhere near the first place by dark. I'd better say goodbye to the others."

She hugged me for a few extra heartbeats and finally let loose. I opened the door and glanced at the rest of my family. On the couch, Libby held Hope, rocking her back to sleep. Beside them stood Violet, refusing to turn and look at me.

"I gotta go," I said quietly. Leaning over the couch, I kissed Libby on the cheek and softly kissed the top of Hope's head, breathing in her baby scent.

"I'll be back in five days or so, Libby," I said to the frowning child. "You help take care of Hope while I'm gone."

She nodded, sniffling back a tear. I turned to Violet, who was still facing away from me.

"You take care of Daisy while I'm gone," I said, placing my hand on her shoulder. "Don't let her get all in a tizzy if I'm not back right away. I promise I'll be back."

Most likely, the teen was crying. But I couldn't tell, because she refused to look at me.

I gave her a few minutes but nothing changed, so I turned

and left. That was the way she wanted it.

Outside I gave Daisy one more hug and kiss. Wilson approached with his right hand extended.

"Good luck to you, son," he said, looking none too happy himself. "Don't worry about a thing here. I'll still be around whenever you get back." He wiped away a single tear. "Godspeed, Bob. I know it ain't easy, but I believe you're doing the right thing…just so you know how I feel."

One last goodbye with Daisy and I made my way to the road. I refused to look back one last time. I was coming back, then I could stare at the cabin for the rest of my days.

I was five minutes down the road when I heard it. I paused, fearing trouble was approaching from behind in the dense fog. I heard the slap of footsteps running up behind me. When I turned, the person nearly tackling me was Violet.

"I'm sorry, I'm sorry!" she cried, hugging me tightly. "I didn't mean anything I ever said. Not the bad stuff at least." Her words came out rushed.

"I don't want you to leave," she begged. "But I know you have to go. And I don't want you to think I don't care."

She kissed my cheek several quick times, pulling my face towards hers and kissing me again on the lips.

"I'm sorry that Daisy won't say it, but I will. I love you. I love you so much. I don't want you to get hurt. I want you to come back in one piece. And we'll work it out when you do come back. I won't be in the way of you and Daisy, I promise. Just tell me you love me or at least care about me. That's all I want to hear and I'll let you go."

I stroked her dirty tear-stained chin. "In some weird sort of way Violet, I do love you. But it will never be the same as between Daisy and me. It just can't be. I hope you understand."

She squeezed me tightly. "I do," she whispered. "I just wanted to hear you say it, even if you didn't mean it. Please be careful, please come back. And if you get all shot up, I promise to take care of you again. Just please come back."

I rubbed the top of her head and kissed her forehead one last time. "I'm coming back," I said, summoning the best smile I could. "That's a promise. Then we're all going to spend a lot more boring years together. Maybe even find you a real man who will take care of you and Hope."

I let her kiss me again, though my eyes did peek back down the highway to be sure Daisy hadn't followed.

She pushed my chest lightly. "Go then. Get this over with. And let's get on with our boring life."

I was 40 feet down the road before I turned to look back and wave. There stood Violet, sobbing, doing her best to wave goodbye. I was glad to have her blessing.

Day 1,100 — continued

An hour plus of walking and I began to feel the effects of my hike. My feet were sore. That may have been the fact that the boots I'd chosen were old and two sizes too large. Even the extra pair of socks didn't seem to help.

My shoulders and back ached from the weight of my pack. I hadn't thought I'd packed all that much, but the tender spot on my lower back signaled otherwise.

Another hundred paces and I found a log to take a break on. Pulling the 45 from my back waistband, I studied the road behind and ahead before taking a swig of water. Damn, it was already tepid. Or maybe it was already tepid way back at the cabin.

I pulled the map from my pocket and looked it over. Seven miles up and in on an old logging road. Five miles back to where the second major creek crossed the road. Not some little babbling brook of water, Wilson had warned. These were creeks I was looking for. And according to my strange friend, I'd been a resident of No Where long enough; I should know what a gosh-darned creek looked like by now.

Back on my feet, I tried to figure out my location. I had to be halfway to the first turn-off, I figured. Maybe even almost there.

A little further down the road, reality set in. Standing in the middle of the road, I stared at the charred remains of Lettie's place. I was barely a quarter of the way to my destination for the day.

I trudged on, silently chastising myself. Nothing about this task was going to be easy. Not the hike there, the search, the killings or the hike back. I needed to get it through my head, right then and there, that this was serious business.

A blister brought my hike to another unscheduled stop about a mile past Lettie's. Gingerly, I took my shoe off and discovered a small pebble that had snuck its way in and was causing the angry, red, irritated patch. No actual blister had formed yet, so I decided to rest for a while to give my foot a chance to breathe.

I closed my eyes for a moment. While I believed I was in decent shape, my massive weight loss had caused my muscles to atrophy more than I thought. The sound of crunching gravel made my eyelids flutter open.

When I looked up, my breath caught in my throat. Three people were walking towards me. I didn't recognize them at first, but the woman's smile was familiar.

"What the hell you think you're doing?" one of the men angrily asked. I focused on him.

"Bud?" I asked. My eyes swam with tears as I rose to greet my brother. I looked at the other two. "Dad? Shelly? What are you doing here?" I thought I spoke aloud, but they didn't seem to hear me.

Dressed as if they were going to church, the three encircled me. I found it strange that they didn't offer a handshake or hug, and even stranger that they all seemed angry.

I turned to my father. "Answer Bud's question, Bob. What do you think you're up to?" I'd never seen my father that upset. It almost looked like he was going to hit me.

Shelly stepped between us. "Bob, darling, you can't do this. This isn't what you're about. You're a kind, gentle soul, not a murderer. You have to go back. Maybe it's time you think about coming home."

I tried to speak, but my voice failed me. In front of me stood three people I loved so much. I had a great deal to tell them, so many things to say. But no words came out.

Bud stepped forward, shoving me in the chest. "You know what I think? Do ya, you little punk?" He grabbed my throat and squeezed. "You're already dead. You just haven't realized it yet. Ain't that right, Pops?"

My father looked uncertain about Bud's assessment. "I worried about you a lot, son. A whole bunch at first. Your mother was frantic, knowing you were up here all alone. I calmed her some, but that didn't stop the nagging feeling in my gut.

"But it's been three years now, Bob. You can't come home. There's nothing left for you there. You wouldn't recognize the world you left." Shelly sadly leaned her head on Dad's shoulder.

"You're not dead," he continued, "not yet, at least I don't think so. But you will be if you don't get your head on straight. You can't do this for revenge, son. That'll blind you, make you lose sight of things. You have to do this for the right reason. You have to defend what's yours. You have to take care of it. And you have to do it right."

Shelly stepped in front of my dad. "Daisy's so sweet, and Libby is perhaps the most wonderful child I've ever met. Violet means well, she's just young. And I don't think there's a cuter baby anywhere in the world than Hope."

"But you're a dumb shit, aren't you," Bud seethed. "You think this is all about Dizzy. Well, little brother, that makes you stupid. You don't fight for the dead. You fight for the living, so they can keep *on* living. Do it for your family, Bob. Do this for the people who actually care about you."

"Use your head, son," my father added. Shelly nodded. They all stepped back towards the road. "Take your time. You only got one chance at this. Make it back alive to the ones you love. You're no good to them dead."

Shelly waved as they headed south on the disintegrating blacktop. "I love you," she called out in the happiest lilt I'd ever heard from her. "Remember Daisy, remember Violet, and don't forget the children. They're the ones who need you now. Be safe, darling."

"Try not to get yourself killed, dumb shit," Bud shouted with a smile. He stopped and saluted me. "Be good, little brother. Be good."

Day 1,101

My eyes shot open at the sound of a twig snapping. Bolting up from the dry forest floor, I pulled my gun to an extended position.

Around me, the woods awoke with the sounds and smells of a new day. Soft pinks and oranges swirled the eastern sky. The pines were black and white, not yet reached by morning's first light. Birds high in the treetops sung of dawn's pending arrival.

Behind me, I heard another sound. I spun and leveled the gun in the direction of my attacker. Two dark eyes stared back at if not through me. I recognized the tuft of white above the eyes, the blue-gray circles around his sockets.

"Chester," I whispered. "What the hell are you doing here?"

Taking in my surroundings, I almost expected the wolf to answer my question. Given last night's dream, some might even call it a nightmare; a talking animal wouldn't have surprised me.

I pinched my cheek to be sure I was still alive, wincing at the pain. I'd feared Bud was right, and I had died before I ever began. Fortunately, that wasn't the case.

I made my way to the road. Staring first left, then right, I nodded as if I knew where I was. Maybe I did because as best as I could tell, I was only a mile north of Lettie's.

"Didn't make very good progress yesterday," I said to the wolf, placing my pack on my sore back. "Gotta do better today."

As I headed north, I saw Chester bolt and head south, back towards home. That was for the best, I decided. An extra set of eyes and ears made it safer there.

Several hours later I stood on a bridge, watching a trickle of water beneath. Wilson had spoken of this bridge, the one where I needed to pay attention to the dirt road going west. At least I thought it was.

I marched forward, searching for the next stream that crossed under the highway. When I came to another bridge, I paused. Looking back to see if I had missed something, running my hand through my hair several times.

"It's supposed to be a culvert," I mumbled to myself, "but this is a bridge."

I trudged on, hoping to find the right stream or creek or river or whatever. I had been up and down this road several times in the past three years. Since a whole lot of wilderness up here surrounded us, it always looked the same to me. Never as much as now though.

Cresting a small rise, I peeked ahead on the road. *Damn it, too far*. Off in the distance, perhaps a couple miles away, I could see the faint outline of the tallest building in Covington: the grainery.

Somehow, through no fault of my own, I had missed my turn off. I blamed it on the crude magenta-colored map I carried. Others, if they were with me, would have said I was to blame. Screw them, those missing numbers.

Back I went down the same path recently traveled. No matter what, I would follow the first road I came to. And if it led to the described destinations, so much the better. If it didn't, well, I'd need a new plan.

Day 1,102

The following morning, I woke up beneath a large pine tree some 50 yards from some type of enclosure. Of course I had taken the wrong path the previous afternoon, what else did I expect from myself?

The first road led to a stream that led to a small lake; a body of water with no distinguishable outlet. It was nearly sundown once I came to the second option. Backtracking had cost me much of the day. A ways in on the gravel path, I came across a meandering stream and I staggered in the darkness.

Exhausted and hungry, I decided to stop and set up camp for the night. But I only managed a few bites before sleep overtook my exhausted body. While I'm sure the bugs feasted as I slumbered, I never felt a single one of their bites.

It was still dark when I awoke and surveyed the small light-blue shelter. In the last of the darkness, I couldn't see any light glowing inside. That didn't mean they weren't there; it probably just meant they were all still sleeping…if they were there.

I thought about my dream from the previous night, the one with my family members coming off the road to torment me.

More than likely, it was the stress of the trip that caused it. That, or my extreme fatigue, or maybe my severely insufficient caloric intake.

Whatever the reason, I found myself still mulling over their words. Bud always called me dumb shit, so that wasn't anything new. Dad always advised me to take more time to think things through whenever I had gone to him with any problems. And Shelly wanted me home…just as I dreamed when I was awake.

But Bud's main point still stuck in my head: Do it for them — the living — not the dead. I pictured each of my remaining friends in my mind, my real family now. Dizzy had been gone many months. He was dead the minute the bullet struck his head. Never would he return to us, not on this Earthly plane. Lettie had once said living is for the living and dying is for the dead. That pretty much summed it up, didn't it? I'd better be doing this for Daisy, Violet, Libby, Hope and myself. Because if I was only seeking revenge for Dizzy's death, I was wasting my time.

I stared at the chimney for a while, hoping to see the telltale sign of smoke wafting into the morning air. There was none, no sounds, and more importantly, no horses anywhere around.

They weren't here, I knew. Not now at least.

Deciding to look inside for any signs they'd been there, I rose from my hiding spot and hoisted my pack on my back. Stepping into the clearing, I checked the house one last time.

I felt my eyes roll as the first light of day illuminated the shelter.

"Shit," I muttered aloud, "that house ain't even blue, it's green."

Sneaking up the creek, I noticed another dwelling maybe 50 yards north of my spot. I'd been traveling for a while, stealthily easing through the brush, and using as much cover as I could find.

Coming closer, I saw the small house through an opening.

It *was* light blue, and there was smoke coming from the chimney. This could be it.

Settling under a thick grouping of spruce trees, I surveyed the rundown home, or cabin, or whatever it was. Unlike my place, it didn't have a screen door and the paint on the front door was faded, peeling in some spots. The grass around the home was overgrown and some weeds reached as high as the bottom of the windows. I knew from my own experience that this invited mice in, allowing easy spots for them to sit and chew through any weakness they found. Well, experience and Lettie's stern warnings.

From the sun dully shining off the front window, I could see that it was dirty and looked like it had been years since it was last cleaned. I figured the light blue paint was from years of fading, not an intentional choice by the former homeowners.

I stood there, unmoving, for a long time. An hour, maybe two. Once, almost right away, I noticed movement inside the dwelling. Someone passed near the front window and peeked out. I couldn't see who it was due to the untidy inhabitants.

Other than that, no one came outside. I didn't hear any hooting and hollering like I unrealistically expected from such a rowdy bunch. As time passed, I started to wonder if the people inside were even my intended target.

I tried to crawl through the brush to get a closer look, but I knew if I moved forward, I'd compromise my cover. The best I could do was to shift 30 feet to the east, giving me a look through the front and rear windows at the same time.

More movement. At one point, I counted two bodies. I thought I saw a third, but the dirt might have been playing tricks on my vision.

Another hour and I began to wonder where their horses were stored. I was certain that Wilson said they were still on horseback. That would require horses. So where were they?

I listened carefully, trying to make out any sounds from behind the building that might be from their animals. Save for a few red squirrels fighting and a pair of blue jays calling back and forth, there were no other sounds.

I peered up at the sun that was beaming over my left shoulder. It was a lot further west than I'd hoped it would be. Mid-day had come and gone, and I knew I had another four hours of daylight at best. It was time to make a decision.

I ticked through the clues.

No sign of horses — bad.

Signs of people inside the house — good.

Unable to tell who they were — bad.

I was nearing the end of the third full day of my operation and still had nothing solid to go on — bad, real bad.

Clouds began to pile up in the western sky, blocking the late day sun. Damn it, they weren't friendly cotton balls of white either. They were the dark kind, thunderheads. A low roll of thunder from dozens of miles off grumbled through the woods.

Unless I got that tarp out in the next hour or so, I knew I'd be getting soaked. *Just great*, I thought.

Day 1,103

I hadn't prepared for the possibility of a storm. Rain, I could handle. A little wind, sure. But this was anything but a little rain and wind.

It started with a lightning display unlike any other I'd seen in No Where. The thick, black clouds eventually covered the sky as evening settled in. They hung over the landscape like a dark heavy blanket, bringing nighttime to me and my surroundings. According to my calculations, darkness had arrived a couple hours early.

Was it dark enough not to be able to find my bag? The lightning rippled through the sky, illuminating my surroundings with pulsating clarity. Of course, each bolt brought with it an ear splitting explosion, lasting anywhere from five to 15 seconds.

When the lightning slowed some, the wind began to blow. No longer was I watching the blue house. No, I was sure that the wind would blow it away at any moment, along with my tarp, supplies and possibly me.

Then the rain came. Of course, a storm like that couldn't just spit on me. No, it was as if God himself was directly above me, pouring an endless supply of gallons of water on me for what seemed like hours.

By the time daylight came, I was soaked, chilled to the bone and exhausted. If I had slept at all, it was only for an hour or two.

Maybe Bud had been right. Perhaps I was a dumb shit for doing this.

The house was still there, but I no longer cared. I figured I had two choices: Go up and knock on the door like a lost traveler and see who was inside, or give up, turn around, and head back home to people who loved me.

Naturally, I chose the first.

I was too tired to go all the way home empty-handed. I hoped the Barster gang wasn't there and whoever was had a bed I could borrow for a couple of hours.

Shaking out the tarp, I studied the house. I still didn't see anyone outside. Maybe they'd seen me already and were waiting for me to show my face first.

Or perhaps they had no idea I was there and would be shocked by a knock on their front door. One way or another, we were about to meet.

I emerged from the thick pine cover and took two steps

before the front door burst open, a double-barreled shotgun aimed in my direction.

"What the hell do you want?" someone shouted from inside. *Yeah, they'd noticed.*

I raised my hands and took several steps towards the male voice. "I'm from down the road, half way to Amasa. I'm looking for some friends of mine."

"Well, you ain't got no friends here." I still hadn't seen a face but the gun stuck out a little further, waving in my direction.

"Maybe we could talk for a moment," I proposed, trying to sound as friendly as a guy could with two barrels of hurt pointed at him.

"You got a name?" he asked, and finally I saw an old grizzled face that matched the hoarse voice.

Slowly I dared another couple of steps, keeping my hands held high for him to see.

"Bob," I replied. "Bob Reiniger."

I paused, waiting for a hopefully decent response. But it was taking too long, and I became nervous. I swore I heard him cock the hammers on the old shotgun. *This might not go so well,* I thought.

Day 1,103 — continued

"I don't know no Bob Reiniger," the man said, finally stepping out of the home. His long beard and ragged clothes told me he was one of us; the lost-in-No-Where-for-eternity type.

Smiling as broadly and non-threateningly as I could, I kept moving towards him. The two steel eyes pointed at my head. "I'm not looking for you, I'm after someone else. Maybe you can help me find him."

When I finally stopped walking, we were five feet apart, two if I included the 36 inches of barrel between us.

He glanced around the stock of his gun. "This friend of yours got a name?"

The gun wasn't going down. Perhaps I'd made a gross miscalculation in my plan.

"Clyde Barster," I answered, my hands still held high above my head. "You know him?"

The gun finally lowered to my midsection. I saw his sideways grin. He spit beside himself. Charming fellow.

"I know two things," he answered, setting the wooden stock of the shotgun in the ground. "First, you ain't no friend of Clyde Barster. He ain't got no friends. You're way too decent of a man to be running with an asshole like him." He laughed and spit again.

I was finally comfortable enough with this man to lower my hands to my side. And it was a good thing; I'd begun to lose feeling in my arms.

"And?" I asked. He signaled me to follow him inside the home with a jerk of his head. "You ain't mean enough or nasty enough to be going after him. You'll probably just end up dead like most people who try their luck at it."

Well, this was a man full of information and negative feedback. If it wasn't for the scent of wafting meat cooking inside, I might've just left without so much as a goodbye. But it smelled like pork. Bacon to be exact.

My God, the bacon was good! Almost as good as the three eggs Mr. Felix Wiggle cooked in the grease left behind by the smoky salted pork.

Felix was not my host. No, he was just the companion and personal chef for Arthur Cragun, who insisted I called him Crag. Beside bacon and eggs, they served me actual coffee — Crag had found a stockpile of it somewhere north of Covington — and some sort of flatbread biscuits smothered in raspberry jam.

Neither man was particularly clean, or had any sort of manners, but they were gracious when it came to passing out food. They had my vote for survivors of the year, previously given to Frank, Lettie and Wilson.

Crag and Felix preferred to eat with their hands, even with the milky yellow egg yolks. Crag mentioned something about maybe they could use the biscuits, but decided not to mix egg and jam. Sound decision, I guess.

They refused to discuss Barster, or anything else for that matter, until breakfast was done. Crag's loud, rolling burp was the only signal I needed.

"How do you figure Barster can't be taken?" I asked, licking red seeds from my plate.

Crag pointed a knife at me after he scooped more jam from the squat glass container. "I didn't say he *couldn't* be taken. He can be taken. Just not by you. If you had an army or at least a couple more fellows, you might stand a chance. You, alone? Nah, I don't think so."

Felix had been staring at me skeptically throughout the meal. Slamming his fist on the table, he leapt from his chair. "I know you!" he howled, pointing at me with a yolk-covered finger. "You're that fellow that lives down the highway. Halfway between Covington and Amasa, in the old log cabin."

I nodded, smiling and trying to recall if we'd ever met. "That's me."

"The one with the two wives and two kids." He poked at his friend, beaming with pride at his knowledge.

I raised my hands as they both laughed. "I'm not married to either one of them," I confessed.

Crag tipped his head towards me, grinning through the dirtiest teeth I ever recalled seeing. "You must been a helluva lover to be able to keep up with two women. Come on, tell us who's the best one."

"I'm only involved with one of them, the blonde." Felix nodded as if he knew what Daisy looked like. Crag's grin said he wanted more details. "The other gal had a child with Jimmy Wilson."

They stared at one another as if I'd told them their mothers were the devil incarnate. "Who the hell would screw a half-wit like that kid?" Crag asked, shrugging.

I leaned back in my chair, rubbing my brow. "Can we please get back to the task at hand? Do you guys know where Clyde Barster and his gang are hiding out?"

They gave one another a telling look. Something in the way their faces tensed and came back to mine at the same time told me I'd struck gold. Fool's gold.

Day 1,103 — continued

I crawled through the late summer brush, sweating through my shirt. Pausing for another sip of water, I checked the trail behind me.

I hadn't had a good feeling about any of this since Crag and Felix had enlightened me as to Baster's latest whereabouts. It all seemed too easy.

One minute they were laughing at me, claiming I'd never succeed in getting the drop on the gang. But once they saw I was serious about taking them on for the safety of my family, I had their blessings for my planned attack.

Felix drew me a detailed map to their three last known locations, in pencil no less. Crag told me what the best approach to each place was. In all likelihood, Barster would be in one of these three spots. Best yet, the keys to their treasure trove of knowledge didn't cost me a dime…sort of.

Crag wanted whatever horses survived after I finished killing whoever was left of the Barster clan. Preferably, both he and Felix wanted a horse. I could have one if there was one left over, but they really wanted two for themselves.

And that made me nervous. I felt like they had been

following me for the past hour. Like they were checking up on me. And it really kind of pissed me off.

They fed me well, gave me information and Crag hadn't shot me on sight. I wondered what I had done not to hold their trust so badly that they would follow me. Did they think I was going to stiff them on the horses? Really?

I paused again as I approached the first location. Crag told me he didn't think they were here, but I needed to be thorough and work my way north and west. I was going to make one sweep of the area. If they were here, I was going to find them.

I needed to focus on what was in front of me. Yet again, as I looked back at the trail, watching for movement, I couldn't shake the feeling that someone was there. But every time I checked, it was empty.

Ahead of me was the first potential hideout. It wasn't much, to be honest, just a dingy, rundown hunting shack half the size of my place. Instead of old logs for siding, this place had rough-cut cedar. And it was mighty rough. I didn't believe the siding had seen any care in the last 30 years.

The brush was heavy enough for me to circle the place at less than 50 yards. There was only one entrance and exit, a yellow door in the front center of the structure. At least I think it was yellow. Time had done a number on the once bright door, leaving it a dirty beige instead.

The rear had one small window, the front a larger one. If they were here, they were stuck.

I crouched and began the waiting game.

The front door looked open, maybe an inch. One of the side windows in the front was wide open and the screen hang limply below, pushed in the slight breeze. Maybe someone was there.

Watching for any movement, I took a bite of an apple. When I burped, the taste of eggs and bacon gurgled up, ruining my apple. Disgusted, I tossed it aside.

There was movement behind me, I was sure of it. Were they stalking me while I stalked them? Was it Chester or some other local wolf who was on to me? Whoever it was left my half-eaten apple alone.

The sun sank in the western sky. If I had to guess, it was going on eight p.m., maybe even eight-thirty. But who really cared.

That was the one bright spot of the apocalypse. No one cared about time anymore. Wilson was living proof of that.

He said he'd show up in the morning. Today or tomorrow

should have always been my question. Or, my morning or his idea of morning? As long as the sun wasn't hidden in the west by the trees behind my cabin, he called it morning.

Even I didn't worry about exact time any longer, or approximate time for that matter.

If I did concern myself with such a meaningless thing, I'd be running late on my little hunting party. I thought it was day three, but it could have been day four just as easily.

I was after prey. When I got rid of the vermin, I'd head back home. And barring some unfortunate accident, the only way I'd turn for home and my family was when the job was finished.

The sun dipped lower and the first chill of the evening set in. I pulled a sweatshirt from my pack and put it on, grateful for its warmth. Again, I sensed someone or something was watching me.

I knew it wasn't from the house. It seemed empty, I was sure of it. Plus, the weeds around the door were cut and trampled. All around the front of the house, I could see the long grass had fresh trails cut in by recent footsteps.

Maybe they weren't there now, but they'd be back. So I settled in for a night of waiting.

Day 1,104

I awoke abruptly and was confronted with a shadow standing over me. Someone with a gun, pointed at my face.

She knelt and held a single finger to her lips. "Just get up," she whispered, "and we can wander back a ways and discuss this."

As long as she had the gun, I figured I might as well be compliant. Seemed like the friendly way to respond, one that wouldn't end in my immediate death.

Backtracking several hundred yards, I walked with the long Colt revolver poking in my back. Before she turned me to face her, she grabbed my pack and revolver. When I turned, I was pleasantly stunned at what I saw.

This wasn't an ugly woman, even with my dolled-up Chicago taste. Though her clothes were dirty, I noticed her face and hands looked clean. Though she wore no makeup (and who did nowadays), she still had a natural good look to her.

But the gun was ugly and still pointed at me.

"What the hell you think you're doing, buddy?" she whispered in an irritated voice.

I lowered my hands to my side. "I don't think that's any of your business, lady. Now if you'll just give me my stuff back, I'll get back to my day and you can run along and play old west with someone else."

I reached for my pack, but she tossed it behind her.

"I need an answer because you're really trying to turn my day into shit," she spewed, jabbing the gun in my ribs.

I leaned in towards her face. Only then did I realize she stood an inch or two taller than I did.

"I'm after someone," I answered, probably sounding less pissed than I was, "and you're messing this up. So leave."

She grinned, waggling the gun a little. "You think you can take Clyde Barster and Jimmy Darling that easy? Like you can just sneak up on them and kill them? Like it's no big deal?"

Well, that was sort of my plan. It was a little more detailed than that. But if you broke it down, those were the main points.

"I've got my reasons. And I don't think you have any say in my plan." *There, put that in your pipe and smoke it, lady,* I thought to myself, bemused.

"You're going to get my sister killed," she replied with a pissed off attitude.

"If your sister is one of them, then yeah, she's dying today, too." I mean that's the way it was, right?

She looked down and shook her head. "She's not with them willingly. She's chained to them, but apparently you haven't noticed that."

No, I hadn't. But when you're busy being robbed or threatened at gunpoint, a person tends to overlook those little details.

"So it's Barster, this Jimmy fellow, and your sister," I stated. "Anyone else riding with them?"

Her face drew close to mine and she placed a gloved hand on my chest. "Pack up and leave," she demanded, giving me a surprisingly strong shove backwards. I could tell this wasn't going to resolve itself pleasantly.

"They robbed us. They killed my friend and burned another friend's place to the ground." I moved within inches of her face, almost nose to nose. "Then a little while ago, they hung two fried bodies in front of my cabin and told us to leave." I wanted her to see my resolve. "So I got my reasons to be here. And I'm not leaving until I get what I came for."

I reached behind her, ignoring the gun pointed at my head. "Now if you don't mind, I'll just collect my stuff and get this over with," I added. "If you want to join me, I won't stop you. But I'm not leaving."

She jammed the butt of the revolver into my chest and I winced. "But we're not killing my sister. Got it."

I looked up and nodded. I guess I had a partner. And a sore sternum to boot.

Jean and I waited somewhat together in the brush were I had previously been alone. I say somewhat because it wasn't like we sat side by side holding hands, though she did take my old spot on the log and made me kneel in the leaves.

Getting her name was nearly impossible. I suppose she thought I'd stalk her after this or something stupid like that. All I wanted was a name to put to the face and flowing long brown hair.

Her eyes were a pretty shade of blue, somewhere between light and pale. But they were tired eyes, the same eyes the rest of us had up here. Probably the same eyes found throughout the world if things were as bad everywhere else as they were in No Where.

Her sister, Lucy, was taken about a year ago in a raid northeast of Covington. Jean claimed their hometown was no more than a wide spot on the two-lane road running through it and laughed when I told her I was from Chicago. She didn't realize how lucky she was to be used to living a hard life before all of this. Or perhaps she did.

The day wore on and we waited patiently for Barster to show up. At least one of us waited patiently. She tirelessly spun the cylinder of her revolver like it was some kind of tic. Even my harshest glare didn't slow her rhythm.

"When do you think they should be here?" I asked, trying to end the boredom.

She shrugged, spinning the cylinder again. "Within a day or two," she answered, blowing make-believe dirt from the gun. "They were here a week ago. Then north of here for a couple nights, then north of that for the last four." She pointed at the home. "Here is where they'll stop next."

I stared at the dilapidated faded green shack. "I got all fall. I don't care." As long as I got clean shots at Clyde and Jimmy, I really didn't care how long this lasted.

"Sun's almost down," Jean said beside me, standing from her comfortable spot. "You take first watch and I'll take the late night to morning." She turned and grinned at me. "You got a blanket?"

I gave it to her, but I made sure she knew I was none too happy about it. "Don't drool on it," I chided, turning back to the shitty excuse for a home. "I don't want your spit all over me while I'm sleeping."

Day 1,105

Midday we sat and snacked on whatever both of us had left. Jean's dwindling supplies were much better than what I had, at least in my mind.

My pack had one-half container of dried venison, two small green apples and a handful of shriveled, spongy carrots.

Jean removed several large pieces of semi-stale flatbread from her backpack, accompanied by two flavors of jam. She also produced some dried cubed beef and dried pears. Compared to my stash, hers was like dining at The Ritz.

She asked, so I told her my story while we waited. I told her all of it: Chicago, my job, my folks, my wife. I told her about being drunk when the world ended, which made her smile. I told her about Frank, Lettie, Marge and Nate.

I explained my involvement with Daisy and Libby. That brought a sad smile to her face, one that spoke of her own pain. I even told her about Violet and Hope. I told her the whole story about Violet.

"Sounds like you have a decision to make when you get back," she remarked. "What are you going to do?"

I wrung my hands and grimaced. "I'm going to have to

send her and Hope away to live with Wilson and Lettie. There's no other solution. I can't risk losing a good thing with Daisy. Not for an 18-year-old girl."

Jean looked at me, confused. "I thought you said she was 14?"

I smiled and chuckled. "And now you understand the complexities of Violet. What about you? You got family?"

Her eyes darkened. "Lucy is about all I got left. Mom and Dad died last winter. Both sets of grandparents are long gone. I got a brother, Jackson. He's somewhere in New York, I suppose I'll never see him again."

I gave her my full attention. Her dead expression took a turn for the worse. "You got a husband?"

"Had one," she answered quietly. "He died about a year in. Type one diabetic. He was okay at first. But that went south quickly once the insulin went bad and then dried up."

Her answer came somewhere between matter-of-fact and all out crying. I dared the question I hated most. "Any kids?" I knew better, but had to ask.

"One. She's dead, too. Caught the same fever my folks did." She looked at me and I saw her eyes water. "Madison. She was four."

I rubbed her right elbow. "I'm sorry." A better man would

have said something comforting, something a little more heartfelt. But not me.

"Thanks," she answered quietly. "That's why I got to get Lucy back. She's all I got left." She peeked at me. "Her and Raymond."

I chortled. "You got a boyfriend?"

She grinned and shook her head. "Do I look like the kind of gal who would date a man who goes by Raymond? I don't think so. He's Lucy's man."

We sat silently waiting for something to happen. But nothing happened all day, and by the looks of things, it would be another day before our targets showed up.

She took my hand and interlocked our fingers. "You're a decent man, Bob Reiniger. In a different world, we might have been something." She let the words hang in the still afternoon air.

"But not in this world." I decided to make it easy for her.

She sighed and leaned in. Placing a soft kiss on my lips, she moved my hands to her body.

And for some reason, I didn't fight it.

Day 1,106

The songs of the morning birds in the trees above woke me. I opened my eyes to little slits and noticed the first light of morning covering the forest. Not enough to make out colors, but enough to show me I wasn't alone.

I slid away from Jean carefully so as not to wake her. Stretching a kink from my back, I studied the quiet house across the small opening. *Still no one there*, I thought. Good, it would have been embarrassing to be caught in the throes of passion by the men I was after.

Pulling a spongy apple from my pack, I dared a peek at my new friend — lover, I guess. I couldn't figure what had caused my reaction to her advance, but it had happened. And even in the woods, on a bed of pine needles covered with a blanket I shared with Daisy at most times, it felt right.

I knew I should have felt remorse, but I didn't. I'd cheated on Daisy. Just as I had cheated on Shelly with Daisy. However, in the upside down world we lived in, this was how it was. Tomorrow could be my death day. I enjoyed the moment knowing that another human and I found a connection. And that was special; there were so few connections left to be made in this world.

Our stories were similar. Except Jean knew most of her family, and a lot of friends she later admitted, were already dead. I had no idea. I'd always thought of Shelly still being alive. Same for Mom, Dad, Bud and his family. Now I wondered.

Jean woke a few minutes later, stretching and pulling her opened shirt closed. Her face wore no telltale signs of embarrassment as I snuck one last peek at her smallish bare chest. Making eye contact with her, she grinned.

"I don't suppose you have coffee and a cigarette to offer a girl," she joked. Pulling her hair into a ponytail, she put her brown leather cowboy hat on and adjusted the brim. Man, she was sexy.

I held up my canteen for her. "I got water," I offered, watching her take it from my hand. I noticed a single finger lingered on my hand for an extra second. "As for smoking, never was one. So I don't have any idea what I'm missing there."

She checked the house, nodding at it. "Still nothing?"

I peeked back for another look. "Quiet as can be. Unless they snuck in and didn't want to disturb us last night." I wasn't sure how she'd take the mention of our late day tryst, but her smile grew, so I knew it was okay.

"That was nice," she said, looking away. "But don't be thinking we're going steady now or anything." That caused me to laugh. "Will you tell Daisy?"

Now that was an interesting question. "Yeah," I admitted after some thought. "Eventually. She'll understand. I'm just glad you won't be hunting me down after this."

She laughed. "You got enough women in your life, Bob. You don't need another one." She became serious and more focused on the house. "They should be back today, tomorrow at the latest. What's our plan?"

I glanced back at her. What was our plan?

In the warmth of the afternoon sun, I watched Jean sleep. We had agreed earlier to take turns napping. One person would watch while the other slept. We wanted to be rested when Barster and his man showed up. It was as far as we ever got on our plan.

I listened as Jean snored slightly. It made me smile. Violet too had a cute little snore when she was overtired. Not the kind like my grandfather had, a snore that could wake the dead. Just a cute, little, tiny snore.

Before her turn to nap, Jean snuck to a nearby fast-moving

creek where she filled our canteens and bathed. She didn't tell me she had, but she was gone long enough to bathe. That and the wet hair and glisten of water on her clavicle told me she was clean.

I woke her when my eyes began to become heavy. By the sun, I knew it was late afternoon. Maybe this wasn't the day of redemption. Perhaps it would have to wait until tomorrow.

I would contemplate all of that after my nap.

Day 1,106 — continued

A distant sound stirred me out of my slumber. As I bolted up, a hand covered my mouth, Jean's gloved hand. As I focused on her, she raised a single finger to her lips.

"Shhh," she whispered. "They just got here."

Slowly sitting up, I turned and faced the home in the early evening light. In front of us, three riders dismounted their steeds and stood tightly in a group. Someone was talking, but I couldn't make out what they were saying.

Jean pointed with a shaking hand. "There's Lucy," she said. The girl stood slightly apart from the men, staring at the ground. Where Jean was tall and thin, her sister lacked any height. She was a stolen waif, lost in a forest of madness.

"The taller one is Barster," Jean continued. "And that short, skinny shit is Jimmy Darling."

She said the second man's name with so much disdain that I just had to ask.

"Do you know them both from before?" I asked, staring into her eyes for any sense of recognition. "Or just the short one?"

She remained focused on her sister, moving in small

motions to get a better glimpse through the pine boughs.

"Barster, no," she replied, keeping her voice low so that we remained undetected. "Jimmy I know. I've known him for a long time. And I always thought he was as rotten as he's proven to be."

There had to be more to the story. I sat back and waited for Jean to speak again. She glanced at me with a half-shrug.

"Jimmy's from nearby where I grew up...where *we* grew up." For a moment, a memory must have invaded her thoughts. She shook at one point and came back around. "He was hot on me for a while. But then I got married and he left me alone."

"And then Lucy..." I added, knowing only half the tale. But it made sense, at least to me.

"She was always so sweet, so innocent, so pure," Jean said, sounding sad. "It wasn't bad enough whatever happened happened. Then people started dying and then Jimmy grabbed her one night when she went out for supplies. I knew it was him." She stared directly at me. "It was always gonna be him."

"How old is she?"

Jean sighed almost loud enough for the others to hear her. Luckily, they were too involved with getting the saddles off the horses. "I'm 26, Lucy's 21."

"And her boyfriend has no interest in finding her? Or helping out at the very least?" I probably shouldn't have asked that question. I already knew how Jean felt about her sister's beau.

"Raymond's a coward," she said softly. "I haven't seen him since before she got taken and not a lick of him since. He knows what's happened. He's probably just moved on."

"Maybe he died," I added quickly.

Jean laughed. "Oh, the world should be so lucky." She nodded at the house.

Turning my attention back to my targets, I caught my first glimpse of the chain that held Lucy captive. It looked like an old, steel dog chain. Maybe 10 or 15 feet long, one end wrapped around her neck, the other held tightly by none other than Clyde Barster.

In the low light, I couldn't recognize the man's face, but his distinct voice took me back to when they first robbed us at Lettie's place. A soft ringing in my ears must have meant my blood pressure was on the rise.

"Here ya go, darling," Barster crowed, tossing a gunnysack at Lucy. "Find us something in there to cook up for dinner. And if you behave real nice like, I might even let you have a bite to eat."

I noticed Jean fingering her revolver. "You want to take them now?" I asked.

Her eyes darted left, then right, and finally she looked up. "Too dark, not safe. We'll have to wait until morning."

In front of us, Lucy screamed as Jimmy molested her in plain sight. I felt a lump grow in my throat, and a quick glance at Jean told me she felt the same. Her face tightened to the point where I thought her lips might explode.

"Jimmy!" Barster shouted. "You got all night to do as you please with her. Have her get a meal cooked, then you can have your fun."

I touched Jean's right shoulder and she flinched. "I'm sorry," I whispered, watching her wipe away the first tear I'd seen her shed. "I know this is hard."

She sat back, clenching her fists. "I've been here before. Not this place, but another they use. I was so close to getting Lucy back. But they had an extra man then. He spotted me in the brush and I had to run.

"This is the third time I've seen my sister since she was taken. And every single time Jimmy Darling has his grubby hands all over her." She turned and grabbed my forearm. "He's mine. I want him. I want to cut his balls off and feed them to him while he dies. That's what I want done with that prick."

Raising a hand to my mouth, I tried to hide some of my horror. "How about we just kill him instead? Case closed that way. Plus, we won't have a eunuch chasing after us for the rest of creation."

She nodded once, her face still drawn and tight. "You can kill him, right after I get done with him."

I turned and watched as someone lit a lamp or candle inside. The last we saw of the trio was Barster himself hanging a sheet over the window. That meant no night attack; too risky with a young lady inside who was an innocent.

So we waited, and Lucy's cries haunted our nighttime watch.

Day 1,107

I didn't sleep except for a few winks here and there. I had to beg Jean to close her eyes for a little bit, which she finally did. Neither of us would be any good without a little rest. That actually felt like a recipe for death to me.

We both were wide awake by first light. That was kind of funny, I thought. The house was finally quiet.

There had been a fair amount of commotion during the evening inside the house. As we watched and listened, swatting to keep the bugs at bay, the two men argued verbosely.

"We don't need no more supplies right now," one said in a growling tone. "We got plenty of what it takes to live good for the next week. So drop it." I assumed that was Barster.

"But we need to keep the pressure on that place to the south of here," the second man whined. "We need to drive those people off so we can have that place before winter."

"We'll kill them all come fall," the first man responded. That made my blood stop flowing for a moment.

I felt Jean's hand grip my leg. "It'll be okay," she whispered, trying to sound reassured. It better be okay, that was my life and my family Barster so easily cast aside.

Later, we heard Lucy's screams fill the night air. Occasionally we heard a slapping of skin, followed by wails I knew I'd never get out of my mind. Then that higher pitched voice pierced the night air. "Oh Momma, you're so good. Just like Daddy likes it."

"They'll be dead tomorrow," I said, trying to reassure Jean in the darkness. "It all ends then."

Her only response was a sniffle and a single word, "Yeah."

As the morning wore on, we witnessed Barster walk outside and urinate in the front yard. It wasn't a pretty sight, but I noticed Jean's intense glare held on the man.

"Can you hit him from here?" she asked, nodding at him.

I studied the distance but doubted my accuracy. "I could maybe hit the front window from here…maybe." If nothing else, I was honest.

She checked our surroundings. "We need to get closer, and it'd be best if those two shit heads came outside without Lucy."

Almost as if prompted by her speech, Jimmy Darling wandered outside to relieve himself. Chained to his wrist was a completely naked Lucy. I heard a sharp breath from my companion.

"Why don't you look away?" I asked, diverting my eyes from the emaciated and bruised girl. In dawn's fresh light, she looked tougher than I had expected. Perhaps even tougher than Jean remembered.

"Keep your eye on the prize," Jean whispered back. "My dad always said that was the only way to win."

We both watched as Jimmy pushed her against the side of the house and mounted her from the rear. Finally, Jean looked away. Thank God.

Day 1,107 — **continued**

After sunrise, the group as a whole emerged from the home. Lucy was still in tow, dragged along by the chain around her neck. Thankfully, she had a shirt and shorts on.

They seemed to be discussing water and who should run and get some more. From my point of view, Barster was winning the conversation. Shortly after a shouting match between the two men, Jimmy and Lucy grabbed two pails and headed north for said water supply.

"I say we move now and take Barster while Jimmy's gone," I stated, keeping my voice low.

Shaking her head, I noticed Jean's scowl. "And if anything goes wrong, we run the chance of losing Lucy. I don't want to take that risk."

She studied the house closer. "If we can just get them out here with their backs to us, we can do a sneak attack from the rear." She must have noticed the skeptical look on my face. "At least we can get closer for a chance to shoot, right?"

I nodded, seeing Jimmy leading Lucy back. In her hands were the two buckets. Apparently, their water supply was close by.

The pair disappeared inside, followed by Barster. "Shit," I muttered.

Bad guys one, good guys zero.

By mid-afternoon, the pair made another appearance to pee in front of us. Watching them from our hiding place, I noticed Lucy and her chain were absent. I nodded at Jean, she nodded back.

"I swear you're going to kill that girl," Barster complained, strolling away from us.

Jimmy's bladder must have held more because it was a good half-minute until he finished his job.

"Daddy needs loving," he howled. "And she ain't all used up yet. So when Daddy wants it, Daddy takes it."

"I'm gonna kill Daddy," Jean seethed beside me. "Let's sneak around the edge they're headed for. That way when they turn their backs to us again we can take them."

We backtracked a bit and slid through the woods with fox-like stealth. Even I was surprised at how quiet we were, now that our lives depended on it.

When we crept forward, Barster and Jimmy were directly in front of us, but facing sideways. They spoke in low tones so I couldn't make out what they were saying. Behind them, the three horses ate green and brown late summer weeds, occasionally sticking their heads in a large trough that was most likely full of water.

We waited for our opening…and waited…and waited.

I became frustrated. Right in front of us were the two remaining members of a gang that had harassed my neighbors and me for the past year. I could almost smell the stink emanating off a man like Barster. Just as rotten on the outside as he was on the inside.

Beside him, the weasel-like Jimmy Darling leaned against a tree, picking at his teeth. Either they were ignorant to their surroundings or Jean and I had the drop on them. I wasn't sure the options weren't one in the same.

Barster turned slightly towards the horses and I began to rise. Jean's hand on my thigh stopped me mid-rise. She looked at me and shook her head. Something wasn't right in her mind. I crouched again and we continued our wait.

"Here's what I think," Barster began in an almost civil tone. "That place south of here is good…" He stroked his scraggly beard. "But there's better."

Jimmy took a seat on a nearby pine stump. "Like?"

Barster grinned and I noticed his missing teeth, like every other one.

"That place at the back end of the swamp," Barster said, winking at his partner. "The one with the high fence and that bald shit that shoots first and never asks questions."

Shit, he was talking about Wilson's place. This pitiful man had big plans.

"Now that," Barster said, poking at Jimmy, "that would be a hell of a place to spend the winter. Don't ya think so?"

Jimmy looked deep in thought. "I think we may die trying to take it. I like the place on the main highway. Think they've left by now?"

Barster shrugged. "Don't know. But if we kill that skinny-ass man, we can have it and the two women there. You could replace poor old Lucy if she dies soon."

"She ain't gonna die," Jimmy complained.

"You don't feed her, pretty soon she will."

Jimmy grinned. "She had a little food few days back. She just needs enough to keep going. At least going for my purposes."

Both men laughed and turned their backs to us. I saw Jean rise and did the same.

Go time! I thought.

Day 1,107 — continued

Jean's gun was at full draw as we dashed out of our hiding spot. Mine would have been as well except it got caught on a pine branch at the last moment. A horse threw its head back and whinnied, giving away our sneak attack. By the time I had my 45 up and ready, Jean fired the first volley of our war.

Though we had tried to be as quiet as possible, Barster saw our approach, aided by the horse's whining no doubt. "Look out, Jimmy," he shouted as Jean's Colt released its bullet with a loud percussion.

I saw his arms go up, flailing as the bullet struck home. The scrawny man fell face forward, struck somewhere in the back by a 230 grain 45-caliber hunk of lead. His legs kicked towards us as I watched Barster hightail it around the corner of the house, disappearing from sight.

I shot once, hoping to hit the man; Jean fired three more times. Pausing against the wood siding, I watched as she reloaded her revolver.

"I don't think I hit him," I said, trying to catch my breath. "You?"

She shook her head, spinning her cylinder several times. "I

hit something. But if it was him he should have dropped."

She scowled at the writhing man on the ground at her feet. I could tell she was considering making good on her previous threat.

I laid a hand on her arm. "Don't, we need to find Barster before we do anything more rash."

Still staring at the body, she shook her head. "Okay. Let's get this over with."

Sticking her head around the corner, she peeked once, then twice, at the last known location of the enemy. When I looked at her face, I could tell Jean hadn't found what she was searching for.

"No Barster and no blood," she whispered, looking past me towards the front of the house. "You sneak around back and I'll do the same on the front. Maybe we can trap him."

Hugging the outside wall, I inched along the back of the house. When I got to the window, I knelt to the ground and crawled past, just in case Barster had sought refuge inside. When I got to the far corner, I jerked my head out and back trying to spot him but saw nothing.

Tiptoeing to the front of the house, I leaned around the corner. A figure caught my attention and I leaned back. Whoever it was looked close. I checked to make sure my safety was off, which it was. I flexed my trigger finger. I needed to be ready when the shot presented itself.

Extending my arm around the corner, I peeked at my target again. Shit, it was Jean.

She shook her head at me in a disgusted fashion. "You planning on shooting me?" she whispered loud enough for me to hear.

It was my turn to shake my head. "Sorry," I mouthed. In my defense, I hadn't shot.

She pointed at the front door. I slid my head away from the house and noticed it was ajar. I nodded back at her.

"Nice and easy," I whispered.

She looked at me, perturbed. "Duh."

One cautious step at a time, we made our way to the opening. Jean bent down as she passed the front window. What seemed like an hour later, we stood plastered to the house, each of us two feet from the door.

"Give it up, Barster," I shouted. "It's over. Come out with your hands held high."

Several rapid gunshots sent wood splinters flying through the air as he peppered both sides of the doorframe.

"I don't think he wants to play nice," Jean said, glancing at the door.

"I'll come out, but I got a little present with me," Barster replied, laughing as he spoke. "Back away from the house and stand out in the yard. Straight away from the door."

I knew what he meant and I'm sure Jean did as well. He still held the upper hand and he knew it. We *had* to do as he said.

Standing side by side with Jean, I noticed movement by the door. The first person out was Lucy, the chain still wrapped tightly around her neck. Around her chest was Barster's left arm. To her shaking head, he held a gun…my old gun.

The pair stepped outside into the sunlight. Lucy squinted slightly. All she wore was a dirty button-down shirt and panties. No pants, no shoes, and since her shirt was opened in front, I knew no bra either. Jimmy must have been plenty busy again.

In the light of day and up close, the girl looked tough, real tough. Her face was bruised and unwashed. Her hair looked like it hadn't seen a brush in months. Through the opening in the front of her shirt, I could see bruised ribs. And she had a pronounced limp. A large, black bruise spotted her left foot that looked to be fresh.

Barster hid behind her small frame, tried to at least. While some of his body was exposed, most of his face remained hidden behind Lucy's head.

"Toss those guns down," Barster barked. "Half-way to me. I'll have little Lucy collect them when you do."

I glanced at Jean and sighed. This wasn't good, not good at all. I began to think this was my last day on Earth.

Day 1,107 — continued

Lucy retrieved our weapons. A yank on the chain tugged her back to Barster's side. He inspected the guns before stuffing them in his belt.

"I see you're both packing 45s," he mused, studying Jean more than me. "That's a lot of fire power for little old me and Jimmy. You meant to do us in real good."

His narrowed eyes met mine. "Jimmy dead?"

Refusing to show him any fear, I shook my head in a tiny fashion. "Don't know really. Last time I saw him, he was slithering around in the dirt on his belly. Seemed like his natural environment to me."

Barster chuckled and pointed his gun at me. "Jimmy's a real piece of work, I admit. And if he ain't dead after I kill you two, I'll probably have to finish him off myself."

The reference to killing brought a rise of emotion from Lucy. "Please, Clyde, don't hurt them," she begged, pulling at his bare arm. "Just let them go. They won't come back." She looked at us, pleading. "Isn't that right? If he lets you go, this is all over. You'll never come back, right?"

I shrugged, but noticed Jean stiffen. "I'm here to get my

sister. I plan on killing you and taking her back to where she belongs. That's the only way this ends."

Barster smirked at her words, breaking into a chuckle that became an evil laugh. "Oh, I wondered when big sis would come to save little Lucy. Jimmy always said you were quite a looker. He also said you had a mean streak in you a mile long."

He hooked the chain to a bolt sticking from the siding out of Lucy's reach. Grabbing the sides of her face, he forced her head up. "Don't you do anything stupid now. I need to talk to big sis man to man for a bit. You try to unhook yourself and I'll hurt you worse than Jimmy ever did. Understand?"

Through rivers of tears, Lucy nodded. She tried to speak, but Clyde shushed her before turning his attention on us.

"Kneel, both of you," he requested in a tone that at any other time would have been considered civil. When we didn't comply, he waggled the gun between us. "On your knees, on the ground." He grinned, pointing the gun behind. "Or Lucy gets the first shot."

Begrudgingly, I knelt and pulled Jean down with me. I noticed she looked more determined than scared. And there were no tears. If she were about to die, she was ready to face her maker without giving Barster any satisfaction of emotion.

He approached with the gun at his side. "I was led to believe that big sis was without a man. But here you are and you have one. Interesting what a pretty girl like you can convince someone else to do just by parting your thighs."

Maybe Jean planned to answer the filthy soul, but I didn't. We remained quiet.

He took a stance directly in front of Jean, about three feet away. "It didn't have to be this way. You could have just stayed put and Lucy would have been fine. I wouldn't have let Jimmy kill her. I ain't that rotten."

I saw the corners of Jean's lips curl upward. "Could've fooled me," she replied defiantly.

He moved directly in front of me. I stared him in the eye.

"You, I know you from somewhere," he surmised, scratching his beard as he thought about it. "I'm good at faces. We've met before."

My turn to smirk. "Can't say that I recall."

He nodded several times, bobbing his head from side to side, inspecting my face.

"You're that fool who was living at old lady Hamshire's place," he proclaimed proudly. Damn, he did have a good memory. "You ain't all pissy because we took a little food from you, are you?"

I thought carefully about my reply. If there was the slightest chance of getting away alive, my next words probably dictated my fate.

"You have no idea," I seethed, spitting at his feet.

In all likelihood, I was a dead man. So be it.

Day 1,107 — continued

The menace paced for quite a while. I saw his lips move as he spoke, mostly to himself. Occasionally he went back and tormented Lucy for a moment, only to return in front of us.

"See, I gotta do this," he said, pointing his gun at Jean's head and then mine. "Can't have people chasing after me all the rest of my days. And the way I see it, you," again the gun was at my head, "are probably out for revenge. I don't blame you, I guess."

Again, the pacing began and I grew impatient. "Are you going to try and bore us to death?" I asked in a snarky tone. "Or are you going to be a man and do something? Because I'm getting sick of kneeling before a worthless piece of shit like you."

He grinned before he spoke. "If I could trust you, I could let you go. But I can't trust you not to come after me again, can I?"

I didn't bother to dignify the stupid question with an answer. I just stared at him and he stared back.

Moving in front of Jean, he stroked the top of her head. She pulled away, disgusted by his touch. Grabbing a handful of hair, Barster jerked her forward again.

"Maybe I'll kill Lucy and keep you around for fun," he sneered, licking his lips perversely. "Jimmy pretty much used her up. I ain't interested in second-hand sluts. What would you think of that, darling?"

Jean glared at him. "I'd rather be stripped naked, have my guts cut open and left in the middle of the road for the wolves to feast on while I was still alive. Your touch repulses me. You make me want to puke just by being in your presence. You keep me and I'll hang myself on the dog chain before you ever get a taste of me."

His evil grin made me shiver. "I think I'll take that taste right now. See if you're worth keeping around."

"No!" Lucy shrieked. "Leave her alone, Clyde. I'll be good, I promise. Just let her and that man go. You won't come back, will you Jeanie?"

A huge lie might've come in handy right about then. But for some reason, neither Jean nor I were able to hide our true feelings.

"I'll hunt you down like the filthy pig you are, Barster," Jean growled. He backhanded her and knocked her to the ground.

"Get your shirt off," he barked. "Let me see what you got so

I can decide who dies today. You and him..." he pointed the gun at my head, "...or him and your sweet little sister."

My head swiveled in Jean's direction. "Don't do it," I stated in a plain tone. "Don't give him the satisfaction."

Jean stared into my eyes, trying to say something without words. What was she trying to convey to me? It will be okay? I have a plan? Or maybe, today's a good day to die.

"I have to," she whispered. "I have to do it for Lucy. Don't let her die, Bob. Please don't let her die."

"Shirt, off!" Barster barked, causing Jean to flinch.

She turned and faced him. "Okay, I'll do it. But you gotta let Lucy live. Deal?"

He drew a deep breath and nodded at her. "That could happen. Let's see what you got and maybe I'll let you both live. But the man dies, today."

Jean looked back at me, tears filling her reddened eyes. "I'm sorry, Bob. But you know this is about Lucy, not you, right?"

I tried to give her a comforting smile to show it was okay, but a single word was all I could muster instead.

"Yeah." I was going to die. But maybe they'd both survive, somehow.

"I got a bad shoulder," Jean said to Barster. "I need Bob to get behind me and help me take my shirt off. All right?"

Barster's eyes shifted between us. If he was trying to decide whether to allow it or not, he sure was taking his sweet time. I guess it extended my life expectancy by a minute or two, so I didn't complain.

"Okay," he agreed. Smiling, he placed the barrel of his gun — my gun — against my forehead. "I'm sorry you won't get to see the show, Bob. But you're probably a gentleman, I imagine. A little modesty for the woman is probably proper. Get behind her but stay on your knees. No funny business, otherwise I shoot you both."

I tried to decide whether being non-compliant was worth it. He'd probably just kill me. That would leave Jean alone to do her best against him. Chances were all of us were dead by sundown. Though I knew I'd never see another sunset again.

I nodded in compliance and crawled behind Jean.

Day 1,107 — continued

Kneeling behind my new friend, or lover, or whatever we were, I tried to recall which was the bad shoulder. That's what didn't make sense; I didn't think she had one. However, as she peeled her right arm from her shirt, she pointed at the left.

"Don't raise it up," she said. "It might make me pass out from the pain. Just slide it down."

Completely confused by her words, I began delicately sliding the shirt away from her left side. Her bare torso caused Barster's grin to grow.

"Bob," Jean continued, "there's something stuck right at the belt line in the middle of my lower back. It's been digging in for the past hour. Will you pull it out please?"

Okay, I thought. If she was going to be naked, she may as well be comfortable. I leaned back slightly and let my eyes slide down her slender back.

And there it was…hope.

Noticing Barster's interest piqued, I fiddled on the ground desperately, searching for something to show him. I found a hunk of tree bark and held it up, halting his approach.

"Oh, that was a nasty piece of crap caught in there," he

said, looking down and smiling at Jean. "Must have got caught in there when you two snakes were slithering around in the brush, trying to figure out a way to kill me."

He leaned closer to Jean, reaching for her chest. "How'd that work out for you, sweetie pie?"

Behind him, Lucy tugged desperately on her chain. "Leave her alone, Clyde. Please, leave her be."

He turned, laughing at Lucy. That gave me the chance I needed to retrieve what was really digging into Jean's back: a small, dull, black handgun.

Barster was busy shouting at Lucy. I leaned in close to Jean's right ear.

"Does it have one in the chamber?" I asked in a breath.

She nodded slightly. "Just flip the safety off. But be sure he's clear of Lucy before you take a shot."

Barster turned and saw us mid-sentence. He approached too fast for me to make a move.

"Secrets will get you killed, you two," he laughed, pointing the gun at Jean. "You probably need to stand up now so I can see the whole package. I hate to make a deal without inspecting the goods."

Neither of us moved and he stepped closer.

"Can she have some water?" I asked, placing my left hand

on her bare shoulder. "She said she was about to pass out from the sun and heat. I'm afraid if she tries to stand, she'll collapse."

He considered the request, his face twisting with each thought. He turned and walked directly at Lucy, taking any shot away. Nervously, I fingered the trigger behind Jean's back.

He unhooked the chain from the wall and led Lucy to the doorway. "Go inside and grab that pail of water," he demanded. "And be quick about it. I got other stuff to take care of today besides babysitting your sister."

Lucy disappeared inside and Barster stared after her. As silent as possible, I stood and raised the gun at the man. He might have been 20 feet from me, probably no more though.

"Barster," I shouted, causing him to spin. When he saw the gun, he raised his own but I got the first shot off.

Splinters of wood kicked up from the house next to where he stood and he fired at me. Damn it, I'd missed. Just before he managed to get that shot away, I dropped to the ground, covering Jean.

"Get him," Jean seethed below me. I rose and saw Barster running towards the right side of the dwelling.

He was maybe 10 feet from the corner when I drew a bead on him. Lowering the sight to center mass, I released a second shot while he was still five feet from safety. He shrieked and reached for his leg. Bingo!

I saw him flop on the ground just around the corner and waited for him to return fire. Two quick shots sailed past, missing me by a wide margin. He couldn't see me, but I could see his legs. He was down and scrambling to get up.

Rounding the corner, I shot him again in the mid-section, causing him to drop his weapon. His hands searched for the Glock, but I kicked it away. Taking him by the injured leg, I drug him back in front of the sisters he had tormented for long enough.

This ended now.

Day 1,107 — continued

Seeing Jean and Lucy reunited, hugging in tears, I stepped on Barster's free hand. The other looked mangled, like he had fallen on it. Not that I cared.

"That first shot was for stealing from us," I vented. "The second was for Lucy."

I pulled the trigger again and a small caliber bullet buried in his waist. "That's for burning Lettie's house down." Another shot to his right shoulder. "That's for those people you burned to death."

I pointed the gun at his groin and jerked the trigger. He let loose a primal moan that probably sent animals for miles around into hiding.

"That's for threatening my family." I knelt on his heaving chest and aimed at his forehead. "And just so we're clear on this…this one's for Dizzy."

His face went confused; his head shook wildly. "That's what this is all about? A piece of shit like him? You're an idiot for revenging another man's death. Especially that turd, Dizzy. Tell me that's what this isn't all about? Tell me you got a lick of common sense in your brain, boy?"

The last shot ended any further conversation from Clyde Barster. He shook for a few seconds before his eyes rolled back. Then he was no more.

"That's exactly what this was all about," I spat between gritted teeth.

Later, I drug Barster's body back by Jimmy Darling. He too was dead. A single shot, most likely from Jean's Colt revolver, ended his life. She told me she was glad he had to lie there and suffer for a while. Made everything right in her mind.

Spying something rusty and dull in the dirt, I picked it up. My Glock. I shoved it in my back pocket; happy to have it back where it belonged.

With their arms wrapped around one another, Jean and Lucy sat on the ground in front of the dingy house, recalling events since their separation. Most of the day was gone. I wondered if it would be better to shack up here for the night and head home in the morning or start now and stop somewhere along the way if needed.

"We're taking off in a little bit," Jean said when I asked her what she wanted to do. "There's three horses back there, so we'll each have a ride home."

She noticed my silence. She hadn't seen what I had when I

dragged Barster back to join his old pal Jimmy.

"Slight problem there," I began. "Seems like we shot two of the horses. One's okay, but the other two are dead. Sorry."

Jean slapped her forehead. "I knew I hit something when Barster ducked around the corner. I just didn't think it was the horses." She grinned at me. "Got a coin? We can flip to see who gets it."

I smiled and stared into the late afternoon sunshine filtering through the trees. *A little breeze would have been nice,* I thought.

"You take it," I replied. "I got 10 miles, and you told me earlier you have 20 to cover. I'll be fine."

"You can come with us, if you'd like," Lucy offered kindly. "We could use a good man back home."

I winked at her. "I've got a home and loved ones to get back to. They'll be looking for me. A couple of them will be pretty damned worried, I suppose. But thanks."

I helped them load up supplies from Barster's hideout and watched them ride off into the proverbial sunset. It would have been into the actual sunset, but they headed northeast.

"You take care of yourself, Bob Reiniger," Jean called out, waving one last time. "If you ever get sick and tired of that Daisy woman, you know where to find me."

I only waved; no more words were needed.

Turning east towards the road, some four miles through the summer woods, I began my trek home.

And I never planned on leaving again.

Day 1,108

After spending the night in a completely run-down shack, I started back on the road a little after sunrise. I had hoped to make it all the way home, but fatigue — caused by not eating much the last few days — caught up with me. I slept like a baby that night. Even the grotesque amount of bugs in the place didn't disturb my slumber.

Meandering down the middle of the deserted road, I passed Lettie's old place. I wondered how the old bird was doing back at Wilson's fortress. More than likely, she had that group of men saying please and thank you in every sentence. She always figured a little bit of discipline and a whole lot of manners went a long way.

I was three miles from home. Relief flooded over me as I reflected on my time away. This was the tenth full day since I'd left. I hoped they'd be as excited to see me as I was to see them. All of them.

Recalling my dream from many days back, I snickered. Bud was wrong. I could do what had to be done. I *did* do what had to be done. Now we were safe. Maybe safe for the rest of time.

As I walked the last few miles, I allowed my mind to

wander. I thought about Shelly. In a silent prayer, I wished her the best. We would never be together again. Not on this Earth at least.

Mom and Dad came to my mind. I wondered how proud my dad would be if he knew all the things I had accomplished. If he realized, against all odds, I was still alive, with no plans of dying anytime soon.

Daisy was at the forefront of most my thoughts. The life we'd made together so far was nothing compared to the eternity we'd spend with one another. Libby would be our daughter until someday she had to plant us in the ground, or maybe feed us to Chester's descendants.

We had to deal with Violet and Hope, but no time soon. After the days I'd been through, I figured I could put up for a while yet with whatever Violet tossed my way. By winter, I decided. By the time the first snows came, they'd have to move out of our home and in with Wilson. It was the only logical solution.

Frank and Dizzy were the only ones lost thus far. Not bad considering the world we knew was long gone. Each day was a struggle just to survive. But I'd done better than survive lately. I had defended my home, my family, my friends from the evil lurking outside our very front door. I could see Frank and

Dizzy's smiles. I could almost hear their words: *You done good, Bob. You done good.*

Ahead, a figure appeared on the road. As I stopped and studied it, I realized it was coming closer…running. I reached for my weapon, checking the chamber to be sure it was ready if needed.

A few more seconds and I recognized the long hair flapping in the wind. For a moment, my heart skipped a beat.

"Daisy," I muttered, picking up my pace to greet my love.

A few strides later, I realized the hair wasn't blonde. And I saw the form was taller and thinner than Daisy. I stopped hurrying and waited for the girl.

Violet.

Day 1,108 — continued

She hit me at a dead sprint, leaping at the last moment, wrapping her thin arms and legs around me. She damn near knocked me backwards onto the pavement.

"You're back!" Followed by a kiss on the lips. "Thank God you're safe." Another kiss, again on the lips. "I was so worried about you." This time, Violet gave me a more passionate smooch and I let it go on just long enough to satisfy her. When I set her down, I saw tears.

She had to know that this was the end of us. We could never be anything more than friends. That had to explain the tears and worried look.

"I know I was gone a while longer," I said as she played with my hair and then my beard. She still had the damned worried look. "But it's over now. It's done, we're safe."

Her head shook and she looked back in the direction of the cabin. Something was wrong.

"What is it?" I asked, starting to get that funny feeling in the bottom of my gut. She bit a nail, staring at me for a moment and turned away again.

I grabbed her by the shoulders to face me head on. "Violet,

what is it?"

She began to weep and buried her head in my chest. That really made me worry. Did something happen to Hope while I was gone? Maybe word came from Wilson about an illness that had taken Lettie from us? Or somebody could have had an accident with the ax or one of the guns.

"Tell me what's wrong, Violet," I demanded, pushing her to arm's length. "You need to tell me what's going on!"

"Someone came, a few days ago," she sobbed, grabbing at my shirt, trying to pull herself closer. "They came and we weren't ready. They surprised us, even Mr. Wilson."

My stomach felt lodged in the middle of my throat. I had to clear the phlegm several times before I could speak.

"Who came?" I asked, loud enough to startle the girl. "Who exactly came?"

She looked at me, frightened. Was it the news she held ransom, or me, I wondered? She nodded in a tiny fashion.

"Those people," she cried. "Those people from Covington. I'm so sorry but they caught us so off guard. Even Mr. Wilson didn't see them until it was too late. I'm sorry, please forgive me."

I shook her; I didn't mean to, but I did. "What did they want, Violet? What did they do?" My words were angry. Any other time, I would have felt bad. But not then. She needed to level with me. Something big had happened and I didn't have a clue.

Her eyes rose slowly to meet mine. "I tried to stop them. I promise you, I really tried to stop them. There were eight of them, and they had guns pointed at us. They wouldn't listen. I'm so sorry."

She paused and I waited for her next sentence. I knew they had killed someone.

"They took her, and we couldn't stop them. We tried, but we couldn't. I'm so sorry. They took her."

I shook her hard, upset with her vague ramblings. "Who the hell did they take, Violet?!"

Her shaking hands rose slowly to her lips. I saw her fingertips tremble as she began to mouth the words. Her crying intensified. "I'm so sorry, Bob. I did everything I could. But they took her — they took Daisy."

We sat at the table, four of us. Wilson beside me, Violet with a heartbroken Libby on her lap across from me. I was so upset with her, Violet, that I wanted to hurt her. She wanted this; this is what she had prayed for. It was all her fault. I just knew it.

But the voice of reason, Wilson, said different.

"It was later in the day, two days back," Wilson started, shaking his head. He blamed himself, and thus far, I hadn't told anyone I didn't blame them. "I took Libby down the road to pick berries, just around the corner. When we came back, there were six of them in the yard. Two more stood in the brush just to the north. If I had seen them, it could have turned out different.

"They would have shot me and Libby where we stood if I would have dared to raise my gun. They made that plain as day. They brought Violet and Daisy outside to join Libby and me. I guess the baby was sleeping." The pain in his voice told me Violet's story was mostly true, though I still didn't want to believe a single word of it.

Wilson rubbed his bald head before continuing, "They were after her, Daisy; even told us so. She was the only reason they came. Seems they had to settle a debt with a fish camp. And they needed an experienced person. And they knew all about Daisy's past experience at a camp. I guess you all know how much Susan Weston hated Daisy. How badly she wanted to stick it to her; even this one last time."

"I told them to take me," Violet desperately added. "I begged them to."

I cocked an eye her direction. "Yeah, I bet you really tried your damnedest." After all, she had received her wish. Daisy was gone and she remained. But I'd move heaven and Earth to change that before the first wet snows of fall came in the next several months.

Wilson laid a hand on mine. "She did, Bob," he replied in an honest, sincere tone. "She told them she was younger, could work harder. Susan Weston laughed at her. Matt grabbed Daisy and said she was coming.

"Violet begged and pleaded. I didn't want either of them to go. But it was obvious to everyone she wanted to go in Daisy's place," Wilson finished and I looked the teary girl in the face.

"Why?" I asked.

Violet became serious, dropping the finger from her mouth. "You know why," she answered quietly. "You didn't want me here. You wanted her. Anyone could see that. In the end, I just wanted what was best for you. I knew if Daisy was here and I was gone, you'd get on just fine."

"The Weston's wouldn't go for it," Wilson continued. "When they started to leave, Violet ran in front of them and dropped to her knees. She begged them to take her. Matt Weston told her to move. When she refused, he put a gun to her head. Said something like, 'Just give me a reason to pull the trigger.'"

He paused and wiped his forehead with a red handkerchief. "Daisy saved her, of course. Told Violet it had to be this way. Told her it would be okay. Told her to take care of herself and Libby...and you."

I sighed and looked between the two. All this time, Libby had been quiet, letting Wilson and Violet tell their story without so much as even a whimper.

The small child looked at Violet in a pathetic fashion. "Do you know when Momma's coming back, Vi?"

Violet hugged her, rocking her gently in her arms. "I'm sorry, sweetheart. I just don't know."

I glanced at Wilson. "Any idea where?"

He shook his head. "Last I heard, there were more than 100 small and large fish camps set up on the south shore of Superior. Likely, it's one here in northern Michigan, maybe the far east side of Wisconsin. But that only narrows it down to 50, maybe 60. At least within two or three weeks' walk."

Placing my head in my hands, I let out a low moan. The woman I loved, the woman I adored, the woman who made me whole, was missing.

I had no idea where to find her. Or even where to start. No Where took on a darker aura at that moment, one I wasn't sure I'd ever be able to shake. Not until Daisy Vaughn was back by my side.

############

Thank you for reading my latest creation.

If you enjoyed *Defending No Where*, please consider going to Amazon and leaving a review.

I appreciate your support.

e a lake

Other Books by e a lake

This is e a lake's entire book library at the time of publication, but more books will be coming out in the near future. Find out **EVERY** time lake releases something by going to ealake.com/contact and filling out the contact form at the bottom of the page. In the comment box, simply state "Add me to your email list." Sign up today; all people on my list are eligible for my monthly prize drawings.

WWIV - In The Beginning

WWIV - Hope in the Darkness

WWIV - Basin of Secrets

❖ ❖ ❖

WWIV - Darkness Descends (The Shorts - Book One)

WWIV - Darkness's Children (The Shorts - Book Two)

Stranded No Where (Book 1: The No Where Apocalypse)

Surviving No Where (Book 2: The No Where Apocalypse)

Coming Soon:

Searching No Where (Book 4)

About the Author

e a lake and his wife reside in Woodbury, MN; just a mere ten minutes from downtown St. Paul. He has three grown children (all married), and four grandchildren.

Sign up for lake's newsletter at: ealake.com/newsletter

Follow lake's weekly blog at: http://ealake.blogspot.com

Follow lake on Social Media:

Twitter - @ealake5
Facebook - ealake5
Google+ - +EALake

Thank you for reading my novel.

Made in the USA
Middletown, DE
05 September 2020